Barry J. Calve
adult club La Chambre remains the biggest such club in the country. He and Marie still regularly appear on TV and take part in radio shows to discuss the swinging scene. Barry's interests, apart from swinging and writing, include art, music and football (although it's just watching these days, unfortunately). Barry and Marie have two grown up daughters and four grandchildren, and live in a quiet North Derbyshire village, where they enjoy nothing better than walks in the countryside with their grandchildren.

BARRY CALVERT

SWINGERS 2

Matador
9 De Montfort Mews
Leicester LE1 7FW, UK
Tel: (+44) 116 255 9311 / 9312
Email: books@troubador.co.uk
Web: www.troubador.co.uk/matador

ISBN: 978-1905886-654

Typeset in 12pt Bembo by Troubador Publishing Ltd, Leicester, UK
Printed in the UK by The Cromwell Press Ltd, Trowbridge, Wilts, UK

Matador is an imprint of Troubador Publishing Ltd

To Danny and Sue – friends for ever

CHAPTER 1

Primitive Lust

I had never seen breasts as big as these, they were huge pendulous things that swayed from side to side in unison as she walked, and due to the earth's gravitational pull on large objects, her nipples pointed permanently south. The shear weight of flesh stretched the skin at the top of her chest into sinewy strands flattening the top and ballooning the bottom of each massive mammary until they resembled two plastic shopping bags filled with water. It was almost as though they had taken her over, that her torso and legs were just a vehicle to carry these two colossal breasts.

She was not particularly attractive, her hair was mousy and without style, her legs looked far too skinny and her bottom a little too big, but none of that mattered with boobs this size.

I had spotted her the moment we had arrived at the house party. Our hosts Mike and Jan were a couple we had swung with before and they had invited us along to their middle class semi on the outskirts of Nottingham. They held these parties about four times a year and spared no expense, a sumptuous buffet was provided and bottles of champagne lined the kitchen worktop, with numerous crates of larger and soft drinks cooling on the back patio. It must have cost them a small fortune but their parties were legendary, and much sought after events in the swinging world, and we felt privileged to have been invited. It was March 1986, we had been swinging for almost six years and were fairly well known in the scene.

It was a much more parochial and secretive pastime in those days and couples quickly became categorised on the grapevine, we were known as players which was a complimentary term as other couples became classed as timewasters, watchers or mickey mousers (couples who wanted to swing but never dared). As players we were in the top echelon of swinging society, and as such, received invites to parties like Mike's and Jan's. It was a title we had earned. Since our first tentative steps into wife swapping, we had seen and done many things, taken the bad times with the good and survived, we had served our apprenticeship and had evolved into confident swingers who could be relied on not to stand in the corners at parties, or bottle out at the last minute. We had also gained a reputation as soothers, a term seldom heard these days, but back then was swingers terminology for a good couple for first timers to meet. We had never forgotten Robert and Helen who were the first couple we ever had sex with, they were our soothers and we had vowed to treat any first timers we met in the same slow sensual and erotic way we had been treated on our first time and sooth the transition.

Since becoming swingers our lives had become paradoxical, we were now living two lives. For ninety percent of the time we conformed to the expectations of society and were the perfectly normal family, for the other ten percent we were swingers and tossed conformity to one side. We were different people as swingers, we spoke in a different way, dressed differently, even thought differently. We were totally unrecognisable as the ordinary couple who did normal family things throughout the week. It had to be that way, we loved our family life, it gave us stability and a solid safe existence in a loving environment, but we needed something more, swinging gave us excitement, adventure and danger. It was impossible to marry the two, so we lived them both side by side, but quite separate. In a strange way each life complemented the other, looking back I don't think we could have sustained either lifestyle if it were not for the other. We never mixed them, never confused them, they were totally diverse and totally segregated, but also inexorably bound together somehow, two completely different entities forming one complete existence. That's how it was for us, that's how it is for the vast majority of swingers, a life of contrast, and this house party would typify that paradoxical lifestyle before the night was over.

Marie, along with the rest of the women at the party, was giving the boob lady venomous looks, she was now stripped to the waist having released her monstrous mammories from the captivity of her immense bra and was dancing seductively to the sound of a motown record.

"Just look at her" said Marie. "They're horrible, far too big, look how they wobble, how can anyone think they look good?"

"Yeah, right," I answered. I had only half heard her, I was too busy trying to figure out how I could get my hands on those huge breasts when every other guy in the place was trying to do the same; it was not going to be easy, she was already surrounded by half a dozen guys who all wanted to make it with her, and I was no exception. As I said, she wasn't great looking or witty, and there were other women at the party who had better figures, but she had a truly mountainous bosom, and sometimes, for a man, that's enough.

I decided to get some info on the boob lady from Mike, our host. "Don't know much about her Baz," he said. "Friends of friends, like, but they're supposed to be players, and what a tremendous pair of tits."

"Hadn't noticed" I said.

Mike laughed, "So it's her personality you're interested in, eh?" he asked.

"That's right" I said. "I just want to talk to her, you know find out what makes her tick."

"Then grab her tits" he said.

"Yeah, something like that" I answered. We both had a laugh and Mike wished me luck before he disappeared upstairs with a petite blond.

Marie reappeared at my side. "Let's have a wander upstairs and see what's going on" she said. I looked over at the boob lady; she was still dancing but was now encircled by at least eight or nine men.

"OK," I answered, figuring that I may get my chance with her later on.

Marie led the way up the thick carpeted stairway. At the top of the landing three bedrooms led off in different directions, all the doors had been wedged open and we could see piles of bodies on the beds, some were moving, some just lay panting, others just watching, it was a scene we had seen many times before, been part of many times before, but we had become tired of group sex. It was fun in a helter skelter sort of way but we now found it too rushed and frantic. We had done it, enjoyed it, but had moved on.

In another room, which looked to be the master bedroom, there were two women giving a show of sorts on a king size bed. One of them had a vibrator that sounded like a lamberetta on full throttle, and every time she inserted it into the other woman the sound would turn into a muffled buzz. I leaned close to Marie and whispered "Now you see it, now you don't, now you hear it, now you don't."

Marie dug me in the ribs with her elbow, but I could see she was trying not to laugh. She quickly led me out of the master bedroom into a much smaller room with only a single bed; there were already two couples in the room making out, one on the bed and one on the floor. Marie slipped out of her dress and began unbuckling my belt, we had just sat down on the floor when the couple on the bed sat up and smiled down at us.

"Would you like to swap?" asked the guy. His wife looked across at me and smiled, she had big brown eyes and a mass of black hair that looked tangled and wet with perspiration.

"Is there room on the bed?" I asked.

"We'll make room" said brown eyes.

I glanced at Marie. She was looking at the guy; he was a good looking bloke with a muscular body, so I wasn't surprised when she said, "We'd love to join you, thanks."

It turned out to be a bit of a muddle on the single

bed, but it ended up with me and the other guy laying on our backs with his feet next to my head and mine next to his, that way the two girls could sit on us and kiss and fondle each other at the same time, a total turn on for all concerned. Brown eyes certainly knew her stuff, and it wasn't long before she had me jerking to an eight out of ten climax. I always hated coming too soon as it meant I had to sit it out for the next twenty or thirty minutes until the urges built up again. So I left the three of them on the bed and went and sat with my back against the wall just watching and thinking.

My thoughts drifted back to that afternoon and my other life when I had taken the kids to Bramall Lane to see the match while Marie did her shopping. By sheer coincidence I found myself sitting next to an old friend I had not seen for about ten years. Snowy, as we had nicknamed him because of his light blond hair, had been an old drinking buddy of mine who I had lost contact with after I had married. During half time we began to catch up on each others' lives. Snowy told me about his wife of seven years and their two kids. He told me of his home and new job as a rep for a pharmaceutical company which kept him busy, and how he looked forward to going fishing at the weekends. We reminisced about old girlfriends, and he confided that about three years ago he had an affair, but had to bring it to an end when his wife came close to finding out.

"But you know Baz," he said, "it was the most incredibly exciting time of my life. I have never felt more alive than those three months I was seeing Jill, and the sex, Baz, now that was something else – it even improved my sex life at home because I was on such a high." He stopped for a moment and surveyed the muddy turf of Bramall Lane, as a frown creased his forehead and his eyes clouded. "But all good things come to an end. I didn't want to lose Angie and the kids, so I said to myself, enough is enough. Snowy boy, you've had your fun, now it's time to live like normal people and stop all this nonsense."

He took a deep breath and cleared his throat. "Good crowd in today, around eighteen thousand I reckon."

"Probably nearer twenty" I answered, feeling a little embarrassed by Snowy's obvious distress. He nodded.

"But you know, Baz, it still hurts. I miss the excitement and the exhilaration of it all, and the sex, oh God, I really miss the sex. I know I shouldn't be laying all this on you mate, you and Marie are probably as happy as pigs in shit, and good luck to you. Christ, you must wonder what I'm going on about, but unless you've experienced it you can't understand." He looked down for a second as though brushing some unseen dust from his trousers.

"Anyway, here's me rambling on, what about you, what have you been up to these last few years?" Before I had time to answer, a huge roar went up as the players took to the field for the second half. After the match I shook hands with Snowy and promised to keep in touch. As I watched him walk away I noticed a hunch of his shoulders that was not there in the old days, and his once luxurious blond hair was now thinning and turning grey at the sides. He was only thirty-six, the same age as me, but he had the posture and disposition of a man of sixty.

I was still lost in thought trying to imagine what it must be like to have a fishing trip as the high point of my week, when brown eyes brought me back to reality by sliding down my body and performing mind blowing oral on me. At that moment I resolved that if I ever saw Snowy again I would sit him down and tell him that both he and his wife could enjoy the excitement and exhilaration that he spoke of without resorting to affairs or clandestine meetings.

It saddened me immensely, and still does to this day, that Snowy and many thousands of men and women just like him live out their lives never pushing their own boundaries, never stepping over the line, never fulfilling their own potential, and possibly worst of all, never experiencing true freedom of choice, whether it be sexual or otherwise.

For most people, pushing beyond the socially accepted limits is taboo; they see it as being too radical and extremist. But swingers have learned to embrace the paradoxical lifestyle, they see it as a measure of life, a barometer of experience. They welcome the contrast and make it work for them, just as we did, and still do.

As the night wore on the party began to thin out, and towards around three in the morning there were only about five or six couples and a single guy left and we all gathered in the lounge for a last coffee. I was pleased to see the boob lady and her husband were part of the group. Although I was sure my chance to have sex with her was gone, I could at least talk to her and perhaps set a meeting up for another time, but when I saw her husband my heart sank. He was a small, thin, weasely looking bloke with a Hitler moustache, and I knew Marie would not fancy him, so a future swinging session was out of the question. But what the hell, I walked over to the boob lady and introduced myself. I told her that I had been admiring her breasts all night but had not had the chance to talk to her before now because of the crowd of guys that had surrounded her for most of the evening. She laughed and explained that it was always the same at parties, but would I like to fondle her boobs now. I looked around feeling a little conspicuous, there were only around a dozen people in the room and the atmosphere had calmed considerably from the hectic free for all revelry of earlier. Mike had dimmed the lights and put on some relaxing mood music, it felt almost tranquil to be amongst people who had spent their sexual energy and were now in that wonderful mellow state of being that can only be achieved after a damn good sex session.

The smell of freshly made coffee drifted from the kitchen as the boob lady put her arms on to my shoulders and linked her fingers behind my neck.

"They're very sensitive" she whispered. "Men have been grabbing them all night; it would be so nice if you just caressed them gently." All eyes in the room were on me and I could feel the expectations from the others.

Marie walked up to us and purred, "Go on Barry, it's what you've wanted all night." She then moved slowly behind the boob lady and reached around very gently stroking her nipples. "See, this is how you do it" she whispered. The boob lady gave a sharp intake of breath and held it for a few seconds then exhaled groaning softly; good old Mike had turned the lights even lower and had began to scatter a few cushions onto the lounge floor, he was experienced enough to know when there was a show in the offing.

Marie was now nibbling the boob lady's neck as she

ran her fingertips softly over the huge expanse of skin of each boob. Following Marie's lead, I reached up and as softly as I could began stroking each breast from the top to the bottom, ending at her nipples, which I caressed between my forefinger and thumb.

All this time the boob lady had been slowly and rhythmically gyrating to the music and moaning softly, but now she began to pant in short sharp bursts. Marie had moved around to her side and had bent down to suck on one of her giant nipples. I obligingly did the same to the other. This had the effect of sending her into some sort of spasm as her head shot skyward, and she let out what I can only describe as a howl of pleasure after which she began to shudder and tremble.

It was clear she had been roughly manhandled all night by the hoards of men, but was now experiencing the kind of delicate sex play she really craved. Because her breasts were so massive, most guys just wanted to grab and paw them – they had mistaken big for insensitive.

Marie had known better – she knew just how the boob lady wanted to be touched, and had led the way, and were it not for her intervention when the boob lady had invited me to fondle her breasts, I am not sure I would have responded in a delicate enough way. But irrespective of how I might have reacted, I was now reaping the rewards of patience. Mike, bless him, had produced a bottle of warm baby oil and was now trickling it over her breasts and down her deep cleavage; another two women and a man had now joined us in gently massaging baby oil into her colossal bosom, and she was beginning to go weak at the knees. After a minute or two she lay down on the living room floor and began to writhe with pleasure. There were now at least seven pairs of hands kneading and caressing her body, and all the time her husband just sat there, never getting involved, seemingly quite content to watch her have fun.

Then without warning she screamed, "I want a prick, give me a stiff prick!" She was running her hands up the inside of her thighs and bringing her knees up as though she was aching to have a man inside her.

"Someone shove a prick into me for God's sake" she groaned. None of the other guys were making a move so I concluded I was the man for the job, so I positioned myself between her legs and entered her as slowly and delicately as I could, trying to keep the mood soft and sensual.

"No, no," she screamed, "harder, I want it harder, slam it into me!"

Now call me an old cynic, but I'm of the opinion that women can change their minds ten times a day and still make you feel guilty that you did not know exactly what they wanted at each change.

"Shag me hard, hard, hard; I want to feel you all the way inside me" she gasped. Who was I to argue? So I began pumping away like a demented jack hammer; the boob lady was screaming like a woman possessed, and the rest of them were rubbing and squeezing her body like crazed bakers kneading a giant slab of dough... and still her husband just sat there with his hands on his knees, not saying a word. I had a tremendous rhythm going now, and was slamming into her so hard there a resounding slap every time I bottomed out.

It had all become very frenzied again, and I noticed

that one of the guys who had been massaging her boobs was now stood up and wanking furiously next to my head. Without breaking rhythm I growled at him, "Hey, pal, if that thing goes off in my ear you're fucking history." It did the trick, as the guy redirected his aim and within seconds had ejaculated over the boob lady's ample bosom.

The atmosphere in the room had now become intensely sexual; the whole group were moaning, shouting and grunting. One of the other women had already screamed to a climax just watching and playing with herself. I noticed others in the group grabbing and pawing at each other, their eyes ablaze with lust as they tore clothes from their bodies and indulged in unrestrained animalistic coupling – we had abandoned any pretence of finesse.

It was, and still is, the most intrinsically and unashamedly lustful sex session I have ever been involved in. It was almost primal in its intensity, pure unadulterated animal lust, all subtlety and sensitivity had gone, to be replaced by brutish, crude and vulgar sex... we were all horny as hell.

The boob lady herself was working up to a monumental orgasm and, as I exploded inside her, she finally reached her own pinnacle. Her body convulsed and bucked so much she managed to kick over a nearby coffee table, sending the table lamp crashing to the floor. Another of her convulsions propelled her hips upwards so violently that I was thrown sideways and landed heavily on my hip. I carried the bruise for weeks.

It was a fitting finale to a session that will live in my memory forever. This night epitomised the paradoxical lifestyle and how two extremes can sometimes work together to make a special moment. It had all began as a soft, gentle caressing with no other expectations than perhaps a relaxing sensual massage, but it had turned into the most primordial and unrefined encounter we have ever experienced. We had all travelled back along Darwin's path, back to the fundamentals, to encounter again the elementary urges of basic, lustful, grunting, screaming sex.

It took about ten minutes for everyone to return to normal, and then uncontrollable laughter seemed to infect us. Looking back, I think the laughter was in part a reaction to the acute embarrassment we all felt at our reversion to the Neanderthal mentality. We had, for a time, become cavemen and women again, and had savoured every minute.

I believe modern men and women still carry the urges deep inside to experience sex at its most basic level. Much of today's sexual experience is either too sanitised or stigmatised to fulfil those primitive needs, and we all sometimes yearn to sample the unfetted lustful abandonment of primitive lust.

We did not set out that night to achieve it. I don't think its possible to plan it, it just has to happen naturally, but once in a while if the conditions are right, it can break through the shield of civilised behaviour and, for a brief moment, we can all indulge our primitive side.

Half an hour later we all went our separate ways, the boob lady and her small, timid husband left quietly; the guy who had almost cum in my ear left looking sheepish, the other couples all departed back to their other lives.

Marie and I said our farewells to Mike and Jan and

headed off through the darkness.

On the way home, Marie said that the girls both needed new shoes for school, and not to forget the dentist appointment on Wednesday afternoon. I had on my mind a couple of phone calls I had to make to suppliers, and a trip to Leicester to pick up more stock. The metamorphosis had gone full circle; by the time we reached home, dawn was breaking. We were back in our other life, just another couple who go shopping and take the kids to the match on a Saturday afternoon.

CHAPTER 2

The Devil Dog

The first chill of autumn was in the air. I pulled the zip of my jacket all the way up and buried my hands in the pockets trying to find the last remnants of warmth for my fingertips to feast on.

"Hurry up" I shouted. As usual Marie had forgotten something and had run back into the house leaving me huddled against the cold at the bottom of the drive. We were on our way to buy a birthday present for Sue, and it had been Marie's idea to walk down to the shops on the High Street.

"It won't hurt us to leave the car for once" she had said, but as I stood waiting for Marie to re-appear I felt the bite of the North wind cut through my jacket and the half mile trek to the shops began to seem less and less appealing.

Finally Marie re-emerged from the front door.

"Thank God," I said, "I'm freezing out here – what have you forgotten this time?"

"These," she answered jangling the car keys in front of my eyes.

"Ah can't take the cold eh?" I said taking the keys from her hand.

"I was just thinking of you" she answered with a half smile.

"Yeah, sure you are," I said as I unlocked the car door and climbed inside. It wasn't much warmer inside the car, but at least we were out of the biting wind.

The car itself was an old mark two Granada estate, a huge hulk of a thing that belched blue smoke and drank petrol at an alarming rate. We had bought it for its cavernous interior and we'd pack it to the brim on our visits to the back street shoe manufacturers in Leicester and Northampton.

Old Smokey, as we had nicknamed him, was a real workhorse; although he always seemed to be on the brink of blowing a piston, he never let me down and always managed to trundle home no matter how much weight he had to carry. I was certainly glad of him now.

I coaxed the big three-litre engine into life, three turns, a splutter, a cloud of blue smoke and we were on our way.

"What are we buying for Sue's birthday?" I asked.

"I thought some expensive perfume or maybe some sexy undies, what do you think?" asked Marie.

"Sexy undies sound good."

"I knew you would say that" said Marie.

"Well then why ask!" I answered.

"Because I live in hope that you can get sex off your brain for one minute" she sighed.

"Look I'm a guy, it's my job, okay?" Marie smiled and shook her head. "Anyhow," I continued, "I was only thinking of you. Sue will turn you on by wearing some nice sexy underwear, you always say making love with another woman is best when you can strip her slowly."

"Barry we're talking about Susie Q here, she will have me undressed and spread eagled on the bed before I have a chance to strip her, slow or otherwise."

"Point taken" I said. "Expensive perfume it is then."

We were driving to Danny and Sue's that night and staying over, just as we had done dozens of times over the past four years. We had almost become like one family, we were as close as any four people could be. For me it was like having two wives, and for Marie two husbands and of course Marie and Sue had the added bonus of both being bi; on occasion the girls would force Danny and I to go out to the pub or a football match so they could enjoy themselves in private without us "ogling them", as they put it.

But it wasn't all about sex, that would give a false impression of our relationship – we were also there for each other in times of need. I remember one time when both Marie and I were bedridden with a particularly bad dose of the flu; without hesitation, Danny put in sick leave at his job, Sue farmed out their two children to her mother, and they both spent a week running our business and nurse-maiding us until we were back on our feet. They were putting in twelve to fifteen hour days to keep us afloat; they never asked for payment, they just got on with it.

As I've said before, for two couples to hit it off and become as close as Marie and I were to Danny and Sue is an incredibly rare thing. Of all the many hundreds of couples we have swung with over the last twenty-two years, there are perhaps only a dozen who we call close friends, and of that dozen, only three couples have ever come close to reaching the kind of relationship that we had with Danny and Sue.

Ironically this trip to the shops to buy Sue's birthday present would bring about a chance meeting that would eventually lead to us forming our second great friendship. Fate has always played a huge role in our lives; time and time again it has forced us onto roads we would not normally have taken. It's sometimes said that we are all masters of our own destiny. I very much doubt that. I think most of the time we just have to play the hand that life has dealt us, the only choice we really have is whether we play it with passion or not.

As I swung 'old smoky' left into the high street, followed by the customary cloud of blue smoke, I never suspected fate had again conspired to throw us another curve. Marie pointed to the chemist.

"Pull up over there," she said. "I'll nip in and see of they have any nice perfume." I dutifully parked up outside the chemist and Marie went inside. We had not travelled far enough for the car heater to have warmed up, so I pulled my jacket collar up and stuffed my hands between my legs thinking how good Sue would look in sexy undies, and wishing I had not conceded so readily to perfume. I had been sitting only a minute or so when a small silver car turned and parked up in front of me, and out stepped an attractive red head in a nurse's uniform.

I recognised her immediately as someone I had seen at a house party about three weeks previously. She had been there with her husband. Marie and I had both commented that they were a good looking couple, but somehow we had not got around to talking to them on the night so we had assumed that our chance to make contact was gone. But now here she was, standing about ten feet away and fumbling with her car keys trying to lock the driver's door. What should I do? Should I approach her and introduce myself, or would that be too embarrassing for her... would she recognise me? We had made eye contact two or three times at the party, but now we were out of context, this was our other life, perhaps she would not be able to put a time and a place to me even if she did recognise my face.

She was still struggling to find the car door key from a huge bunch of keys, and the obviously cold fingers were not helping. If only Marie would come out of the chemist now she would have to walk past her and surely recognise her and say something. But no, she had only been in the shop about three minutes, and I knew from experience that she needed at least five minutes in a shop to get warmed up and even then she would emerge and announce,

"There's nothing worth buying," so I knew I could not rely on Marie's emergence any time soon; no, I was on my own, time was running out fast. She had at last found the correct key and was locking the door, that's when fate stepped in a second time and lent me a hand, she glanced around for a second to see if anyone had seen her fumbling with the keys, and as she turned in my direction she saw me and turned away but instantly looked back again. There was no doubt that she had recognised me, but would she remember where? I took a chance and wound down my side window.

"Hi," I said. "I think I know you," being deliberately non-committal.

She smiled. "The party; we saw each other at the party" she said confidently while walking over to my side window.

"That's right" I said relieved that she remembered. "We never got the chance to talk, what with one thing or the other."

"Mostly the other," she laughed. She was even more attractive close up. Her hair was a deep auburn, her eyes dark blue and she had high cheekbones that gave her a slightly oriental look. She was around her early thirties and had a girlish charm that I found intriguing.

"You're a nurse, I see."

"Yes, I work at the private hospital at the end of Dalewood Road, it's mostly ingrowing toenails and hernias, nothing very exciting, although we do have a few cosmetic surgery patients in now and again."

"Do you do massages, because I have this terrible ache in my back" I said.

"What you need is a full body massage. I'll be glad to give you one" she answered. She looked down and held my gaze for a few seconds before breaking into a smile, she was definitely giving me the green light.

"I'm sorry, I'm being rude" I said. "You must be freezing out there. If I give you our number maybe you and your husband can give us a ring and we can all get together sometime?"

"We'd love to" she answered.

I hastily found a scrap of paper and a biro which I had to shake a few times because of the cold to make it work and scribbled down our phone number.

"Thanks" she said taking the paper and folding it neatly before slipping it into the hip pocket of her uniform. "By the way, my name is Rachel" she said holding out her hand.

"Pleased to meet you, my name is Barry" I answered

shaking her hand. "We'll speak again soon I hope."

"Very soon," she stood up and blew me a kiss before walking off with a deliberately accentuated wiggle of her hips. I watched as she disappeared into a crowd of shoppers, just turning once with a small wave before disappearing from view. I became aware that I had the beginnings of an erection.

"Rachel" I muttered to myself, "you are one horny lady." A couple of minutes later Marie came out of the chemist minus the perfume.

"I couldn't find anything decent in there; it looks like being sexy undies after all," she said.

"Good," I said. "Today just gets better and better."

Marie looked at me. "What are you smiling at?" she asked.

"Remember the house party we went to about three weeks ago, the one in Chesterfield?"

"Yes" said Marie.

"Well, remember the couple we were eying up all night?"

"You mean the good looking guy with the redhead?" said Marie.

"Yes, remember how we never got round to talking to them or even getting their telephone number? Well I've just been talking to her. That's her car parked in front." I sat back waiting for my congratulations from Marie.

"Did you get their number?" she asked.

"Er, no I gave her ours."

"Well, where do they live?" she continued.

"Um, don't know, I didn't ask" I mumbled.

"What are their names?"

"Her name is Rachel" I said triumphantly.

"What's his?" snapped Marie.

"Er, don't know, I forgot to ask," I answered, my voice trailing away to nothing.

"So let me get this straight" Marie said. "There's this great looking couple who we really like the look of at a party, but because of circumstances we never got any info from them, and we think our chance has gone forever, am I right so far?"

I nodded.

"Good. So, then, by a million to one chance you happen to be sitting here on the high street and she parks up right in front of you, and you manage to engage her in conversation, is that right?"

I nodded again.

"And in that conversation you did not get their telephone number, you did not get their address and you did not get his name, am I correct?"

I nodded.

"May I ask what you did get?" said Marie sarcastically.

"A hard on," I replied.

On our way over to Danny and Sue's that night I could not get Rachel out of my mind; not many women had such an instant effect on me in that way. I chastised myself for not asking for their telephone number and address. As Marie had said, by not having that information I had lost control of setting up a possible meeting. If they did not ring we would never know if they just did not fancy us or if they had lost the bit of paper with our number on it... or maybe just never got around to ringing, it was frustrating and I could not believe how amateurish I had been in not covering the angles when I had the chance. All we could do now was wait and hope.

It was good to see Danny and Sue again, we had not swung together for about ten weeks. We'd already had a couple of get togethers re-scheduled because of minor illnesses with the kids, and then Sue's mum was taken ill, so we were glad to be able to pull it together at last. Sue's birthday had served as a focal point. We had missed their company and vowed to make up for lost time, but as we stepped in the door Danny ushered us through to the lounge.

"Wait until you see what I've got Sue for her birthday" he said excitedly.

Marie and I exchanged looks, we knew Danny too well to expect anything mundane. He had once bought her a two hour drive in a rally car on a circuit that would test even an experienced driver, let alone Sue, who was never over confident behind the wheel. She had tootled around the track at about ten miles per hour – the instructor said that no one had ever gone that slow in all the twelve years the course has been open! Another time he assembled all her family and friends for a surprise birthday party, the only problem was he told everyone to be at the White Heart pub at eight o'clock and Danny had taken Sue to the White Swan. It was only when he walked through the doors and found that no one was there he realised his mistake. He then had to bundle Sue back out to the car and zoom over to the correct pub about three miles away, by which time most of the party were stood at the bar. A few had left, and a couple were playing pool, so when Danny and Sue finally walked in the guests were more surprised than she was. So Danny's record on birthday presents for Sue was less than impressive, and we could hardly wait to find out what mystery awaited us in the living room. At first glance I couldn't see anything untoward, Sue was sitting in an armchair with a sort of sickly smile on her face and a pleading look in her eyes that said "Look what he's got me this time!"

I carried on scanning the room. That's when I saw a huge black woolly dog in the corner – it looked like a cross between a Skegness donkey and a Yeti.

"Well what do you think?" asked Danny. He had a big grin on his face and obviously expected hearty congratulations on this marvellous present.

"Its, er, a big dog" I said.

"Not just a dog" said Danny indignantly. "It's a special dog, it protects women. I got it from a farmer who had trained it to guard his wife and daughters while he was out in the fields all day; got him really cheap too as the farmer was taking on more labour so he would be at home more, so he decided to sell him."

"How did you get him home?" asked Marie.

"In the back of the works van, had a hell of a job getting him in the house, though, until Sue came out and lead him straight in. He's sat in that corner ever since."

"What do you think of your present, Sue?" I asked.

She looked at me and her eyebrows raised. "I'm just the luckiest girl alive" she answered, still holding the sickly smile.

"Well, I like him" said Marie. She went over and began stroking his head.

"Careful" I said.

"Oh it's okay," interrupted Danny. "He won't bite

Marie. He might bite you, though."

"Eh, is he dangerous?" I asked.

"No, no of course not, he only gets nasty if you go near a woman."

"Are you trying to tell me we can't go near Sue or Marie?" I said.

"Of course we can" answered Danny. He hesitated for a moment, then continued in a mumble. "Just don't make it too obvious."

"What's that, don't make it obvious? How else are we supposed to do it?"

"He just needs time to settle in that's all, we'll just have to keep our distance from the girls for a bit until he gets used to us."

Marie was having a great time ruffling his main and tickling his chin and he was loving every moment.

"What's his name?" she asked.

"Kevin" answered Danny.

Marie looked up and burst into laughter. "Kevin, you've actually called him Kevin?" she said.

"Oh not me" Danny said, "the farmer had already named him that so we couldn't change it, he's too old to get used to a new name now."

"Are you sure it wasn't Killer or Carnage or something?" I said.

"No, I'm sure that's what the farmer called him," answered Danny.

"Well he doesn't look like a Kevin to me," I said as I sat down on the opposite side of the room from Sue and Marie.

Half an hour later I decided to make my move. I slowly got up and glided towards Sue, trying not to make any sudden moves. Immediately Kevin glared at me and curled a big hairy lip revealing long yellow fangs.

Danny laughed nervously. "There you see, now that's a guard dog' he thinks you're going to molest her."

"Well to be honest, that's pretty much what I had in mind," I said as I eased myself slowly back into my chair.

"Why don't we all go upstairs and leave Kevin to get some sleep on his own downstairs here?" said Marie.

"It won't work" said Sue. "We tried that earlier and as soon as I left the room he howled the place down."

"Looks like we're stuck here then," I said folding my arms and slumping back into my chair.

Danny was trying to be upbeat, but even he was becoming exasperated by the situation.

"I know what to do" he announced. "Sue can go and fuss the dog while I go and sit with Marie, then Marie can fuss him while you go and sit with Sue. That way, when Marie sits back down Kevin won't have seen us move, but we'll all be sat together."

"It sounds just crazy enough to work" I said. "Let's do it."

So while Sue stood in front of Kevin rubbing his head, Danny crept over to Marie on the settee. When Sue sat back down you could see the look of confusion on Kevin's face; then Marie got up and blocked his view while I went over and squeezed into Sue's chair with her.

As Marie sat down again, Kevin's head was swishing from one side of the room to the other; his clouded brain knew there was something wrong, but he couldn't figure out what.

"You will have to get up early in the morning to beat me ,so you will," chimed Danny, but the battle of wills between Danny and Kevin had only just begun. Before this night was over one of them would become supreme master of the household, and one would be cast out.

At this moment, I would not have liked to bet on who the winner would be.

I was closest to the dog, and as the night dragged on I could see Kevin out of the corner of my eye – although his head was not turned towards us, his eyes were. I could see the whites of them as they watched me. It was unnerving. If Sue and I so much as held hands he began a deep rumbling growl that started somewhere around his lower abdomen and ended as an evil snarl that seeped from his drooling mouth.

Kevin was undoubtedly a deeply disturbed dog with a black heart, and I kept an eye on him keeping an eye on me.

Finally I could stand no more. "He's going to spring, I know he's going to spring" I said.

"No he's not going to spring" said Sue. "He might pounce, but I don't think he'll spring."

"That does it" I said. "We're going upstairs."

"You can't," said Danny. "Kevin will howl the place down."

"Not if Marie is still here he won't" I answered.

"Shit, you're right" conceded Danny. "I wish I had thought of that first."

I left the room followed by Sue. As I got to the door I saw Kevin shift position to glare at Danny, and as we were half way up the stairs I heard Danny say to Marie, "He's going to spring, I know he's going to spring."

Once in the sanctuary of the bedroom I could relax

27

and took Sue in my arms. She was soft, warm and curvy and as we kissed I felt her hand reach for my belt buckle.

"Sue, what on earth are you going to do about that dog?" I asked as she pulled the belt away from the buckle.

"Oh you know Danny," she answered, "always trying to buy me unusual birthday presents. He'll end up taking the dog back eventually." She was now sliding my trousers down over my hips.

"Sure, but when?" I continued. "It's going to put a real damper on our sex lives while it's around."

"Something tells me it won't be very long" said Sue as she hooked her fingers in the waist band of my boxer shorts and pulled them down. "Now you will have to excuse me," she whispered, "it's rude to talk with your mouth full."

She was kneeling down in front of me looking up, her soft brown eyes melting thoughts of big black dogs and cold autumn days from my mind. Looking down at her I could see the arch of her back and the luxurious dark brown hair falling over her shoulders, I felt her warm velvet mouth take me, and just for a moment with her head buried in my groin and my fingers running through her shimmering hair I knew paradise.

But it could not last, nothing so pure and wonderful ever does; something had to spoil it, and that something was a huge woolly mentally disturbed dog named Kevin.

The terrible commotion downstairs made Sue pull off me so quick there was a resounding pop like the cork coming out of a wine bottle. Sue looked up, I looked down.

"Kevin!" we shouted simultaneously. In one mad

scramble for the door I forgot my shorts and trousers were round my ankles and I stumbled forwards, knocking into the back of Sue and sending her plummeting through the open bedroom door and onto the landing, where we crashed to the floor in a tangle of arms and legs.

Marie was just coming out of the downstairs toilet as we reached the bottom of the stairs and looked as stunned as we did.

"I had to go to the loo. I've only been away two minutes!" she exclaimed.

From the lounge the sounds of a terrible battle could be heard, terrifying growls and snarls mixed with screams echoed around the house. The three of us burst into the living room. Danny was backed up against the wall holding a coffee table in front of him desperately trying to ward off Kevin, who was circling him looking for a chance to attack.

"Shoot the fucking thing!" shouted Danny.

"What with?" I answered.

"I don't know. Just get it away from me, it's gone crazy. Throw something at it."

"That would make him even madder," I said, although after seeing the menacing bared fangs and the deranged look in Kevin's eyes, I didn't think anything I did could make him any more unhinged than he was at that moment.

Suddenly, Kevin saw his chance. Danny had lowered the coffee table a fraction and Kevin had lunged at him. At the same time both Sue and Marie had screamed. This had made the dog turn his head as he took off, and he slammed into the wall as Danny threw himself sideways.

Kevin was stunned for a moment; as he bounced off the wall and landed on his back, there was a loud grunt as the wind was knocked out of him. I have never seen Danny move so fast, he was up on his feet in a flash and across the room like an Olympic sprinter.

"Shut the fucking door!," he shrieked as he flew past us. Kevin was already regaining his senses, his legs were thrashing around in the air. I don't think he realised that he was upside down and he couldn't figure out why his legs were going ten to the dozen but he wasn't moving.

I pulled the door shut and the thump on the other side told us that Kevin had found his feet again, although he still hadn't figured out that running head long into solid objects is best avoided.

Danny was extremely agitated and pacing up and down the hallway. "That dog is mad" he yelled. "As soon as Marie went to the loo, it went for me. Jumped right over the settee to get me, it did!"

"What did you do?" asked Marie.

"I battered it with the coffee table, but it just kept coming, I don't think it even felt it." Danny was shaking like a leaf and Sue went to hug him.

"Never mind, sweetheart, even though my birthday present has turned out to be the devil dog from hell and almost ripped you to bits, I'm not angry because it's the thought that counts."

This was typical of Sue; in all the years I have known her I can't ever remember seeing her panic or become flustered and it was just like her to inject humour into a tense situation; in so many ways she is the opposite of Danny – where he is outgoing and adventurous she is reserved and safe, and she counters Danny's eccentricity by her calm and composed approach to life. She is a steadying influence on him, and he a rejuvenating one on her, but they fit each other like a glove, and she had brought a smile to his face now as they hugged in the hallway.

"Why do I always buy you stupid presents?" said Danny. "I always ruin your birthday. I'm just an idiot."

"Oh don't worry, we'll sort it, and I wouldn't have you any other way" answered Sue.

"What are we going to do?" asked Marie. It had gone quiet in the room since we had heard the thud.

"Maybe he's out cold?" I said.

"Yeah and maybe he's waiting for the door to open so he can spring at our throats!" Danny replied.

Danny had a point, Kevin was a very psychotic and deranged dog, but he was also extremely devious. The way he had waited until Marie was out of the room before attacking Danny betrayed his evil genius. Even now he could be laying in wait behind a chair to ambush us if we returned.

"We could poison him?" said Danny.

"You are not poisoning my birthday present, even if he is the hound from hell," said Sue.

"We could drug him then," I said. "Have you still got any of those DF118 pain killers you had after your accident? They will have him out in no time, of course they will also send him into a nightmare world of illusion and nausea, but they will do the trick."

Danny thought for a moment. "No, sorry Baz, I fed the last of them to you, if you remember."

"How can I ever forget" I said. "You almost killed me."

"Don't be daft, man, I've taken more than that for a headache!" retorted Danny.

"But you took yours over a three day period, I had mine all at once," I replied.

"Will you two shut up" interrupted Marie. "We still have to decide what to do about Kevin."

"Do you still have the number of the farmer you bought him off?" asked Sue.

"Yes, it's in my coat pocket" answered Danny.

"And didn't he say to call if you had any problems?" continued Sue.

"Yes," said Danny.

"Well, I think being attacked and forced out of your own living room constitutes a problem don't you?"

Luckily Danny's coat was hung in the hallway and the telephone was situated on a table by the front door. Two minutes later, Danny was on the phone, and thirty minutes later Kevin's previous owner was pulling up outside. His jaunty attitude belied the fact that he had just been summoned from his home at 10 o'clock at night to collect a dog that he had sold the previous day; he was a dapper little man with a flat cap and smiling eyes.

"Where is the owd bugger?" he said breezily, upon entering the hallway. We all pointed to the lounge door.

"He's in there" said Danny "but don't open the door. He'll have your throat, so he will."

The little man seemed unperturbed. "We'll see about that," he said pulling an old leather dog lead from the pocket of his tweed coat.

"I suppose you'll be wanting me to take him back" he said as he looped the lead round the back of his neck.

"Yes please, we can't even get into out own living

room." pleaded Danny.

"Well I won't be able to give you your money back. I did tell you that he only likes women, and was very protective, when you bought him."

"That's okay" said Danny. "We just want him out of the house. We can't handle him."

"Okay, no problem, I'll just have to go in and put this lead on him."

As he went to open the door, we all gave a collective shout of: "Wait!"

"Just give us time to get up the stairs before you open the lounge door" said Danny.

The little man looked bemused as we all scuttled up the stairs and stood peeking over the banister. He shook his head and rearranged his cap and was whistling merrily as he opened the living room door. We waited for the sound of snarling and snapping and terrifying screams, but it never came. All we could hear was whistling a few seconds later the little farmer strolled in to the hallway with Kevin trotting sedately behind him. He stopped at the front door and looked up the stairs at the four of us cowering in the shadows.

"It's okay now, folks" he said cheerfully.

"Oh, thanks for coming out for him" shouted Danny.

"Oh, no problem," said the little man. "It's not the first time. I've sold him about four times already and have had to come back for him every time. Seems like I can't get rid of the owd bugger, see you."

As the front door clicked shut, we tentively descended the stairs to survey the wreckage of the living room, while Sue and Marie set about cleaning the place up. Danny and I went into the kitchen to make some coffee.

"How much did you pay for Kevin?" I asked.

Danny looked sheepish. "Fifty quid, but he was a trained guard dog."

"Yeah, trained to kill," I said. "Don't you realise, that little bloke has already made two hundred pounds on that dog by selling him and then taking him back when the new owners can't cope."

Danny looked despondent. "I'm just a dope, Baz, and that's a fact."

I went over and put a reassuring hand on his shoulder. "Don't be too hard on yourself mate. Like Sue said, it's the thought that counts."

Danny finished making the coffee and we carried it through into the lounge where the girls were just finishing tidying up.

"It's not too bad" said Marie. "Not that much damage except for a small dent in the coffee table" added Sue.

"That's where I whacked Kevin over the head when he went for me" said Danny.

"So from now on he'll hate men and coffee tables" I said.

"To say nothing of walls and lounge doors" added Danny. We drank our coffee and began to slowly relax.

"How about the birthday girl" said Sue. "Does she get to finish what she started?" I went over and took her hand.

"Ready when you are," I whispered. But as Sue and I climbed the stairs to her bedroom I felt a pang of guilt.

I was with Sue, but I couldn't help thinking about Rachel.

CHAPTER 3

Our Second Great Friendship

As usual our visit to Danny and Sue to celebrate her birthday had been an adventure. Danny's purchase of a devil dog as a present for Sue had ensured that we had all experienced an eventful night and had undeniably served to keep us from becoming bored, not that we needed any help in that direction. We had known Danny and Sue for almost four years and delighted in each others company, but swinging by definition is about change and experiencing new situations and people, and my chance meeting with Rachel the previous day had stirred within us the old yearnings. I had sensed chemistry between Rachel and myself in our brief conversation, it had reminded me of our first meeting with Danny and Sue, and I remembered how we had breezed through those first couple of awkward hours when meeting someone for the first time.

Sue and I had clicked immediately as had Marie and Danny. Dare I hope that Rachel and her husband would become as good a friends as Sue and Danny or was I placing too much expectation on them, on what after all amounted to only a little over a minutes conversation with Rachel at the side window of old smokey.

As we drove back along the M18 on that chilly autumn Sunday morning I told myself to be realistic, we didn't know Rachel's husband, it would be too much to ask that he and Marie hit it off the way Rachel and I seemed to have. But as we turned north on the M1 I could not help thinking that maybe, just maybe with a little bit of luck this new couple may turn out to be as much fun as Danny and Sue.

Marie's eighteen-year-old sister Jenny had babysat for us and as we tossed the overnight bag towards the laundry basket and hugged the kids she reeled off the usual list of mishaps and items that we should know about.

"I couldn't get the video to work so I couldn't tape the football, Vicky knocked a glass of orange juice all over one of the cushions so I've rinsed it and hung it on the line, Mandy would not go to bed when I told her so I promised you would buy her a new bike if she went, and someone called Rachel rang."

"What!" I said suddenly taking notice.

"Don't panic," said Jenny, "I was only joking about the bike."

"No, the phone call, who did you say had rung?" I asked doing my best to sound nonchalant.

"A woman called Rachel" she answered. "She said she would call back."

"Did she leave a number?"

"No, just said she'd call back, is it important?"

"Not really she probably wants to buy some stock." I had mixed emotions, I was elated that Rachel and her husband had actually called, but was exasperated that we had missed the call and had once more lost the chance to obtain their number. I again admonished myself for not getting it when I had the chance. Marie gave me one of her knowing looks.

"Not to worry, she will no doubt call back later" I said returning Marie's glare.

"I hope so," said Jenny, "You don't want to lose an order."

"No, we don't," interrupted Marie sarcastically. "They're hard enough to come by as it is." She was revelling in her 'I told you so' attitude. She had been baiting me all day, a little dig here, an innuendo there, letting me know time and again how amateurish I had been in not getting Rachel's details

I'd had it, I felt bad enough without Marie continuously rubbing it in, a surge of anger welled up in me as I rounded on Marie.

"She will ring" I snapped. Jenny looked up shocked, the kids both froze mid play, even Marie looked stunned by my outburst. "And if she doesn't it's her loss" I yelled. Everyone in the room stood open mouthed; they had rarely heard me raise my voice and were taken aback by my sudden eruption. "And another thing," I shouted, "That bloody video is going in the bin."

I drove Jenny home and chuckled to myself on the way back as I recalled the astonished look on Marie's face when I had snapped at her. I am normally very easy going and slow to anger, but it doesn't hurt to keep her on her toes now and again I thought.

When I got home Marie was making dinner and looked a little sheepish, the girls were fighting over possession of a Michael Jackson poster so I busied myself sorting boxes of stock in the garage, which at the time acted as a miniature warehouse. After dinner we all went over to Marie's parents where I was always assured of a lively debate on football, as her Dad was an avid Wednesday fan.

Around six thirty Marie called the kids in from the slide on the garden.

"Come on girls, time to go home. It's school tomorrow," and fifteen minutes later, after the usual protests and complaints the kids were safely secured in the back seat of 'old smokey' and we were on our way home.

"We could have stayed another half an hour, I think I was just getting top side of your dad about the best club in Sheffield," I said.

"No, we have to be home for seven o'clock" answered Marie.

"Why seven o'clock?" I enquired.

"Because people always ring between seven and half past on a Sunday," answered Marie.

"Do they?" I said.

"Oh yes" she answered. "It's a well known fact ninety percent of calls from family or friends on a Sunday are between seven and seven thirty, I read it in a magazine."

"I hope you're right" I said. Marie glanced at her watch.

"Of course I'm right," she answered, "if it's in a magazine it has to be true, doesn't it." We exchanged a smile. It was one minute to seven when we arrived home. The phone was ringing as we opened the front door; it was Marie's mum telling us that one of the girls had forgotten a schoolbook.

"She doesn't need it until midweek, we'll pick it up tomorrow" said Marie. I made some hot chocolate for everyone as Marie got the girls ready for bed and we waited.

Seven thirty came and no phone call, eight o'clock and still nothing.

"So much for the magazine theory" said Marie.

"You can't believe everything you read, give it time," I answered, but I was secretly just as disappointed as Marie.

The hot chocolate having been consumed, I took the girls to bed and told them the mandatory story. I was keeping one ear open for the phone and just as I had tucked the girls in and kissed them goodnight I heard the ring, ring downstairs, I listened at the top of the landing as Marie answered.

"Oh, hi Rachel. Yes, of course I remember you. Barry told me that you had spoken at the shops yesterday." My spirits soared. They had rung at last, I glanced at my watch, almost half past eight – nearly an hour late. I will have to write to the magazine and tell them they were out by an hour, I thought to myself as I descended the stairs. Marie gave me the thumbs up as I passed her in the hallway; I sat in the lounge with the door open listening to Marie's half of the conversation, trying to work out what Rachel was saying in the silences by studying Marie's reactions. She was laughing and joking and seemed to be enjoying the call.

Marie does not suffer fools, and I would have been instantly aware by her manner had she not been totally at ease.

"Of course I would love to speak to him," Marie said. I turned towards the open door and listened hard, Marie was about to talk with Rachel's husband. This was the acid test; if Marie did not hit it off with him then all of this will have been for nothing. I need not have worried, within a few minutes Marie was chatting quite happily and had gone into flirt mode, always a sure sign that she was enjoying herself. After a while she called me over.

"Barry, come and have a word with Dave." I went into the hallway. Marie had a smile on her face and mouthed the letters O.K. before handing me the receiver.

Dave was friendly and easy to talk to, he said that when Rachel had told him that she had run into me at the shops they had been as excited as we had been. They had fancied us at the party and were upset that they had not got our details on the night. But when they had called on Saturday night to be told by Jenny that we were not in, they had become disillusioned because they feared that we were giving them the brush off, and had thought about not ringing back, but had decided to call one more time.

"I am so glad you did" I said.

"You're not the only one Barry," answered Dave, "Because between you, me and the gatepost, mate Rachel thinks you're a hunk." I could hear a squeal of embarrassment in the background as Rachel shouted, "David stop it!"

"I'll put her on," said Dave.

"I'll kill that husband of mine!" said Rachel as she came to the phone.

"So you think I'm a hunk, eh?" I said.

"I may have said something like that in passing," she answered coyly.

"Well I'll let you into a secret..."

"What's that?" asked Rachel.

"I think you're a knockout, and you know what happens when a hunk meets a knockout, don't you?"

"No, what happens?" said Rachel.

"The earth trembles," I said.

"Will you make the earth tremble for me?" Rachel asked seductively.

"Only after I've made your knees tremble." I laughed.

Marie was standing in the doorway with her fingers down her throat pretending to be sick, I had to turn away for fear of laughing. Rachel and I teased each other for another few minutes before I handed the phone over to Marie again for the two women to sort out the meeting arrangements. As I went back to the lounge and flopped into an armchair I felt a warm glow spread through my body. I had been tense ever since I had failed to obtain Rachel's and Dave's telephone number at our high street meeting, and Dave's admission that they almost did not ring again had highlighted how close we had come to missing each other. But our old friend fate had come to the rescue again and I settled back, stretched my legs and let my imagination savour the prospect of our first get together.

CHAPTER 4

A Night to Remember

Marie and Rachel had arranged for the four of us to get together the following weekend and the anticipation we both felt was almost tangible. We sensed, as did Rachel and Dave, that the four of us could have something special and the next few days would be a time of keen expectation for us all.

We had another long telephone conversation with them on the Thursday, mainly to confirm all was well for the weekend, but also to help build a picture of our new friends. We were all eager to know as much as possible about each other before we got together. Rachel and Dave were both on their second marriage, Dave was forty-two, ten years older than Rachel, and had two children from his previous marriage who lived with his first wife.

Rachel's marriage had been a disaster from the start and she had never had children, she and Dave had been together for five years and had gone in to swinging because they had both realised that one of the reasons their marriages had failed was the claustrophobic nature of their relationships. Dave was a manager in a small business that manufactured surgical instruments and Rachel was a nurse in a local private hospital, and the really great thing was that they lived in the next village less than three miles away. They had been swinging for four years on our doorstep and we never knew.

"We have a lot of catching up to do," I said as I spoke to Dave on the phone.

"We certainly do," he answered. "We will see you both on Saturday."

Marie had always preferred older men and Dave, at forty-two fitted the bill perfectly.

"He sounds just your type" I told her. "Eight years older than you, probably very distinguished and undoubtedly sexually experienced."

"You don't have to sell him to me," she said, "Remember, I was the one who first spotted them at the house party in Chesterfield and I liked the look of him then." She came over to me and put her arms around my neck.

"Anyhow, what about you, Rachel is only thirty two, you cradle snatcher" she laughed.

"Hey, I'm only thirty six!" I protested, "Rachel will probably see me as a toy boy!" Marie kissed me on the lips and pulled back, she had a mischievous look in her eye.

"What are you up to?" I asked.

"Oh, nothing," she answered, looking down and pursing her lips.

"I have seen that look before, what are you planning?" I said. She looked up again, slowly; the mischievous look had spread to her smile. "Come on," I said, "You're up to something, what is it?" She looked at me for a few seconds, eyes wide doing her best to seem innocent.

"Well, you know, when I was talking to Rachel earlier..."

"Yes." I answered.

"Well, I just happened to mentioned that I was bi. Rachel said that she wasn't and had never been with a woman."

"I see," I said, beginning to see where this was leading.

"And I just happened to think that I could, er, possibly show her the error of her ways." She suddenly lost the innocent look as the mischievous smile re-appeared.

"You mean you see her as a challenge, and you want to bring her over to the dark side," I said. Marie thought for a moment.

"Yes" she said.

"Is there no limit to your debauchery, woman?"

"No," she said, and waltzed off into the kitchen to make a pot of tea. I had to smile, over the last few years Marie had introduced many supposedly straight women to the joys of sex with another female. The vast majority took to it as if it were second nature. But it has to be approached delicately and with understanding. Marie always took them to a private room for their initiation and would never rush things; she knows how a woman wants to be touched by another woman and would take the time to bring her over slowly and sensually.

"I am only giving them their heart's desire" she would say and always maintained that inside every straight lady there is a bi lady trying to get out.

Rachel, by virtue of being a swinger, was obviously open to new ideas and situations, so Marie visualised no great problems in persuading her to try a bi experience. But Rachel was far from being the shy timid first timer, she was a strong, sexually confident woman and would have a surprise or two of her own for Marie when they finally got together, but I'm jumping ahead.

The plan was to go over to Dave's and Rachel's house on Saturday evening and stay over. As they did not have any kids, it was easy for them to accommodate us, and as they lived so close we had less than ten minutes to drive.

The situation could not have been better and Saturday morning found me uncharacteristically washing 'Old Smokey', I wanted him to look his best when we rolled up outside Dave's and Rachel's house. When I was satisfied that he was as clean as he could get I came back into the house where Marie was packing our overnight bag, when I saw her I felt butterflies in my stomach. I had not felt as nervous as this for a long time, and it took me back to our first meeting with Robert and Helen and how stricken with nerves I became as the meeting drew near. But almost seven years had passed since then, I was now confident and self-assured around women.

I prided myself on being a good lover who knew how to satisfy a woman. Marie and I had met hundreds of couples in that time, and you don't make love with that many women and not learn a trick or two. But here were the old jitters again, and I found myself walking around the house moving things from one place to another and making unnecessary trips to the toilet.

We were scheduled to arrive at Dave's and Rachel's

for 8:30, but at 7:30 the phone rang and I knew immediately there was a hitch, it may have been something in the ring tone, or the fact that something always crops up when things seem to be going so well, but as soon as I heard the ring, my heart sank. It was Marie's sister Jenny; she had called to say she was feeling ill so she could not babysit after all. Marie and I were gutted; we could not believe that we had been on such a high all week only to have the rug pulled from beneath us at the last moment. We looked at each other in dismay, but there was nothing we could do. It was too late to get another baby sitter and even though Vicky the eldest was now eleven years old we would never have dreamed of leaving them on their own, family always came first with us, so there was nothing else for it but to ring Rachel and Dave and cancel, heaven knows what they would think. I dropped into the chair.

"Looks like I'm going to be watching football tonight" I said. Marie sat on the arm of the chair.

"I suppose we had better ring Dave and Rachel" she said looking down at me.

"Go on then," I answered.

"Why me?" said Marie.

"Well, why not you" I said sinking lower into the chair.

"You know them better than I do" was Marie's reply.

"How do you work that out?" I protested.

"Because you have actually met Rachel and I have only spoken to them on the phone."

"What!" I said, "That doesn't mean anything!"

"Well one of us will have to ring them," sighed Marie.

"You know what they are going to think don't you?" I said. Marie frowned. "They will think were putting them off again, but what else can we do?" I wracked my brains for an answer, but came up with nothing.

"Well, we can't just sit here all night," said Marie.

"We will draw straws to see who rings them" I said, Marie gave a groan.

"Don't be silly we can't draw straws. You've been watching too many films" she said.

"Of course we can, it's the only fair way, unless you concede." I looked at her hoping she would find drawing straws too childish and make the call.

"Get the straws," she answered. Shit, she had called my bluff, but I still had a trick up my sleeve. I went into the kitchen and pulled three straws from the drawer. I cut one in half and snipped a bit off another, the third one I left in tact and slid it up my shirt sleeve, that way if Marie picked the longer of the two I had cut I could still hopefully replace the short one with the long one concealed up my sleeve. It was cheating but I really did not want to make the call. I came back into the living room and held out my fist with the tip of the two cut straws sticking up.

"Choose" I said.

"This is stupid," said Marie.

"No its not, it's the only impartial way to decide who makes the shitty phone call," I said, "Now choose."

Marie studied the two tips; she lifted a hand to take one, then lowered it to study them again.

"Come on," I said, "We haven't got all night."

"Don't rush me," she snapped, "I have to think."

"It's only two bloody straws," I said "Just take one."

She raised her hand again very slowly and held it an inch from the tips of the straws, she then glared at me through narrow eyes trying to see if I would give anything away as she neared a particular straw tip.

"It's no good looking at me, I've forgotten which is which," I said.

"In that case, I'll take this one" she said, gripping one of the straw tips between her fingers and thumbs. I knew she had picked the long one, if she pulled it out I would have to distract her somehow, while I replaced the short one in my hand with the long one up my sleeve. We were locked eye-to-eye like poker players in some western movie. Just as she began to pull on the straw the phone rang, Marie immediately let go and went into the hallway to answer it.

A moment later she was back with a huge smile on her face.

"That was our Jenny. She says she's feeling a bit better and if we still want her to baby sit she'll be ok, but you will have to go over and pick her up."

One minute later I was in the hallway fumbling with my car keys to go over to Marie's mums and pick up Jenny. Just as I opened the front door Marie called to me.

"Barry, before you go, why are there three straws on the coffee table, all different sizes?"

"Got to go," I answered shutting the door behind me and scurrying down the drive to 'Old Smokey', I looked back to see Marie standing at the window with a sort of puzzled look on her face. I fired the engine into life and swung off the drive glancing back just once before heading off down the road. Marie was now smiling and nodding.

With Jenny safely in place babysitting, Marie and I were on our way. The drive itself was short; it hardly gave us time to mentally prepare before we were pulling up outside Dave's and Rachel's house. It was a modern detached building in the middle of a quiet residential estate. The house itself was set on a sloping hillside which meant the drive was quite steep and about twenty steps leading up to the front door. As I looked up I saw Dave appear at the window, he gave a wave and opened the front door as we were half way up the steps.

"Ever thought of a stair lift" I joked as I reached the top of the steps and shook his hand.

"You should see it in winter. It's like the slalom at Innsbrook" he laughed.

"Good to meet you at last," I said.

"And you," answered Dave. "Rachel has not stopped talking about you all week."

"Stop it, his head is big enough already" said Marie, as she scaled the top step, dragging the overnight bag behind her.

"And this must be the lovely Marie," said Dave. "You're even prettier than I remembered you at the party."

"I like him already" Marie said, as she kissed him on the cheek. We followed Dave into the hallway where he took our coats and directed us into the living room. The furniture was expensive but not lavish and without the usual clutter you tend to find in houses where there are children.

The large living room window gave panoramic views over the rooftops of the other houses and being so high up afforded the room total privacy without the need to draw the blinds.

As Dave followed us into the room he took hold of Marie's hand and led her over to the window.

"This is the best place in the house to have sex" he announced.

"Why is that?" asked Marie

"Because on Sunday morning you can watch the local pub team play football on the playing fields while having sex doggy style."

"Why does it have to be doggy style?" Marie enquired.

"Because then I can eat a pizza off your back at the same time," laughed Dave.

"At last a man who has his priorities right," I said. Marie and I laughed with Dave. He was easy going and relaxed and I liked him immediately. He was a well-built man with a very slight middle age paunch, his features were square and rugged, he had been an amateur boxer in his younger days and his nose still bore testament to the reason he quit. By his own reckoning he lost a lot more than he won, so he decided to pursue a business career instead, and after many ups and down had become reasonably successful. The twinkle in his eye and his lively personality made him attractive to women and an entertaining friend for a man. Above all Dave was a survivor, the kind of man who, when he is down will just dust himself off, stand up and start all over again.

"Barry I have an idea" he said, "Rachel is still in the kitchen cooking dinner. She doesn't know you're here yet. Go and surprise her."

"I don't want to give her a heart attack," I answered.

"No, she'll love it" said Dave, "Just make sure she

hasn't got a spatula in her hand or you could end up branded," he chuckled.

Dave pointed the way to the kitchen and off I went, creeping down the hallway, wondering if scaring the living daylights out of Rachel was really the best way to announce my arrival. By the time I had reached the bottom I had decided it was not, and thought it best to knock on the kitchen door. Because the house was built on a hillside the kitchen was up three steps, in fact the whole back of the house was higher than the front; it was a novel layout and gave the impression of being on a boat with the different decks. As I climbed the steps and looked into the kitchen I could see Rachel standing with her back to me crumbling something into a saucepan.

She had on a short green dress and high heels, the strings of the apron were fastened loosely around her hips and hung over her bottom. I saw the curve of her waist and wondered how it would feel in my hand, her hair was loose and came to just below her shoulders, a dark red contrasting vividly with the emerald green dress. The radio was playing in the background and she was humming to it softly and singing the chorus line.

I wondered again how it would feel to touch her skin, to put my belly against hers. In a couple of hours I would be making love to this woman sharing her most intimate and vulnerable moments, kissing, touching, tasting her, in a couple of hours we would both enter willingly into a realm where the force of energy is so powerful it's frightening and the intensity of experience is arrow like. I stood, leaning against the door frame watching this stranger in her own kitchen and knowing what we were about to do and I felt afraid just for a moment, I understood the enormity of our lifestyle and the willingness with which we walked into the mine field. I looked back down the hallway, somewhere just a few yards away was my wife with another man, a man whose sole intention was to make love to her, to make her scream with pleasure.

A cold shiver ran down my spine and I suddenly felt like a child in a grown up world.

"Snap out of it," I told myself, "What the fuck is wrong with me? I have done this hundreds of times, so has Marie."

I took a long slow breath and began to feel better, my confidence came flooding back and within a few short moments I was back to normal. These small moments of panic do happen very occasionally, they only last a few seconds, a minute at the most but they can be terrifying while they last. I have tried to analyse why they happen and believe them to be a residue of our indoctrination by society. After all if you have been told for thirty years that something is wrong and then decide to do it, there has to be some psychological pay back. Or it could be that society is right and we should all stick to one partner all our lives, all I know is that as I watched Rachel reach up to take a small bottle of herbs from a shelf her dress rose above her stocking tops and I suddenly felt all grown up again.

"I love the view from this room" I said, lowering my voice in an effort not to startle her too much, she turned quickly and looked at me for a few seconds as if trying to figure out who I was.

"You're here!" she exclaimed.

"Yes, Dave let us in. Sorry if I made you jump," I

answered. "It was Dave's idea for me to creep up on you" I added quickly, I did not want her to think I was in the habit of sneaking up on women, but then blaming Dave seemed as if I was trying to pass the buck. *Well done Barry, great first impression* I thought to myself as I stood in the doorway with an apologetic smile on my face.

Rachel soon regained her composure.

"Don't worry," she said, "He does things like this all the time, I should be used to it by now." She walked slowly over to me untying her apron as she came, "Do you mind if I get something out of the way before we go down to the lounge?" she said, standing in front of me with a serious look in her eyes.

"Of course not" I answered, wondering what she was going to say. She stared at me hard for a few seconds and I began to fear the worst. Then her expression began to soften, she put her hands either side of my head and pulled me down to her lips. We kissed for at least three minutes, open mouthed, tongues darting, exploring, hands caressing, roaming, she tasted sweet, smelt sweet and if it were not for the fact that we were in the kitchen amid steaming saucepans and had to go and join the others soon, I could very easily have made love to her there and then.

As we finally came up for air and pulled away from each other I exhaled slowly.

"Yes, I am, er, glad you got that out of the way," I said.

Rachel looked up at me, her lipstick was smudged all over her mouth, she smiled.

"Now we won't be looking at each other for the next two hours wondering what it will be like to be together," she said.

"Well you certainly know how to break the ice," I answered. She took a couple of tissues from the kitchen drawer and passed me one.

"You're wearing more of my lipstick than I am," she laughed.

We wiped out faces, Rachel applied more lipstick and we made our way down the hallway. We entered the lounge to see Dave laying on the sofa and Marie giving him oral. Rachel stood with hands on hips and shook her head.

"Dave, how could you do this to me, I've been slaving over dinner all day and now Marie is going to ruin her appetite."

"Consider it an appetiser" said Dave between groans. I stood back in awe, this couple were as cool as cucumbers, I had considered Marie and I to be the more experienced couple by virtue of having been swinging two or three years longer than they had, but Dave and Rachel were up there with the best of them, of that there was no doubt, and tonight was going to be akin to Real Madrid playing A C Milan in the European cup, two top teams at the height of their game displaying all the talents and skills at their disposal. Being a football fanatic I have always equated life's experience in footballing terms, I often find it helps my understanding of situations a little better, don't get me wrong, Marie and I have sometimes performed more like Bogend Rovers on a wet weekend but tonight we were raring to go and so it seems were Rachel and Dave. It was going to be magnificent and if there had been a referee I would have been begging him to place the ball on the spot and kick us off.

Dinner was a splendid affair, three courses with all

the trimmings finished off with brandy and coffee. The conversation flowed as easily as the dinner wine, and Rachel and I teased each other outrageously during the meal. It was all a preamble to sex, we knew that and we played it for all it was worth. There was no question of doubt in either of our minds that we would have great sex later, we fancied each other so much and could hardly wait to get down to business. Marie and Dave were just as horny, they had been tossing sexual innuendoes at each other all through dinner and I didn't think it would be long before they resumed their pre-dinner activities. We were all in the living room now just lounging around, relaxing and letting our meal settle. Dave crawled over to the television on his hands and knees and pushed a cassette in the video.

"This is a great film" he said as he crawled back to the settee and sat next to Marie.

"Is it educational?" laughed Marie as the titles began to roll and the familiar cheap sounding music spluttered from the speakers.

"Oh yes," replied Dave, "It's full of human interest. you'll learn a lot by watching this film."

"What's the title?" I asked.

"Pretty peaches."

"Ah an agricultural film" said Marie.

"Well yes, it does get a bit earthy," Dave answered. By now Rachel had come over to sit on my lap and had pushed her hand down the top of my shirt running her fingers through the hairs on my chest and nibbling on my ear.

"So long as it has a story line," I said.

"Yeah, a blue film with a story line is like a woman

with three tits, it's just not needed," joked Dave. But I couldn't answer him, my mouth was filled by Rachel's tongue, we were deep kissing, exploring every exquisite recess of each others mouth, tasting her saliva, running my tongue over her perfect teeth feeling how smooth and even they were. She would dart her tongue into my mouth and I would do he same to her, she was one hell of a kisser, her lips were warm and full as they glided over mine. Time after time she rotated her head searching for the best position for maximum tongue penetration. I could very easily have spent the whole night just kissing Rachel.

It was just so relaxing sitting there with her on my lap and enjoying those luxurious kisses. All thoughts of anything more seemed like an intrusion, I did not want anything to encroach on this moment, neither it seemed did Rachel, we must have kissed solidly for at least twenty minutes. When we finally stopped to quench our thirst with glasses of wine, we both remarked how reddened and sore our lips felt and looked. Rachel took the opportunity to apply more lipstick whilst I poured more wine and watched Dave and Marie making love on the sofa. They seemed to be in a world of their own, completely oblivious to me watching them as they rolled around spilling the cushions onto the floor and groaning loudly.

Rachel finished applying her lipstick and came over to take my hand.

"Shall we go into the bedroom, we'll be more comfortable" she said softly.

"Sounds like a good idea," I answered. She led me out of the living room, past Dave and Marie who were now hanging half off the settee as their passion began to reach fever pitch, past the television where the blue film was only half way through, and out into the hallway. She led me into a bedroom about half way down the hall and closed the door behind us. The room was cool and quiet and I watched as Rachel drew the curtains and switched on the bedside lamp.

I have always considered the moments just prior to making love as the most erotic. The expectation reaches fever pitch and the excitement is electric. Rachel knew exactly how to prolong this moment as she sat on the edge of the bed and very, very slowly removed her stockings and suspenders.

"Give me a hand with my zip will you" she whispered as she stood up with her back to me and looked seductively over her shoulder. I walked over and ran my hands up the small of her back to the top of the zip on her dress and began to pull down as slowly as I could. The dress fell to the floor and I began to nuzzle the side of her neck. She still had her back to me and I now had my arms wrapped around her waist.

As I kissed her neck I slid my fingers down the front of her panties, she had shaved and felt soft and smooth. She began to groan softly as my hands began to caress her pubic area. She reached back and began to unbuckle my belt, her movements had quickened, she spun round to face me, her face flushed, we began to kiss, harder kisses than before, more intense, more sexual than sensual. Soon we were both naked and on the bed, panting and groaning, touching and rubbing, licking and sucking, I was in ecstasy and so was she. It had all fitted together like a jigsaw, and all it needed now was the final piece.

As I entered her she gave a shriek of pleasure and raked her nails down the full length of my back. I arched up for a moment but it gave me such an endorphin rush, I began pumping into her like a man possessed. She responded by wrapping her legs around my back and screaming even louder, we had both lost it. We had entered that small incredibly intense bubble that two people form around themselves when engaging in total sex. Marie and Dave had been there when we had left them on the sofa and now Rachel and I were there too. The bubble only bursts when you climax and ours exploded like a volcano, as we came together in a screaming, shuddering, sweating heap of flailing arms and legs. Neither of us could speak for at least five minutes, we just lay there exhausted, hearts pounding and gasping for breath. Eventually we both tottered off to the bathroom on shaky legs to clean up, and then made our way laughing to the living room, and Dave and Marie.

They were both lounging naked on the sofa and looked ruffled and reddened, we all looked at each other and pronounced in unison, "Wow!"

It had been a truly momentous night and the sex had eclipsed even our expectations. But it wasn't over yet. After a rejuvenating cup of coffee, Marie and Rachel got it together on the sofa while Dave and I watched.

Rachel was showing the same enthusiasm with Marie as she had shown with me. I turned to Dave with a smile.

"And you're sure this is Rachel's first time with another woman?"

"Yes" he answered, "She's been desperate to experience another woman for a long time." We watched Marie and Rachel writhing, kissing and licking for a few minutes and Dave spoke again.

"Do you think she will take to it?" I gave a wry smile.

"Does a spaniel have floppy ears?" I answered, we both laughed and settled back to enjoy the show.

It must have been something like four in the morning when Dave and Rachel finally led us to their guest room and we all wearily said our goodnights. As I slumped onto the bed I began to take off my shirt which I had put back on after my session with Rachel earlier in the evening.

"Christ, I must have had a good sweat on, my shirt is stuck to my back," I said as I peeled it off.

"That's not sweat" Marie exclaimed, "It's blood."

My back was streaked with claw marks, some of which had drawn blood that had dried and stuck my shirt to my back. Marie bathed me with warm water and now that my sexual euphoria had diminished I began to feel the pain.

"Well we know what to get Rachel for her birthday" said Marie.

"What?" I asked.

"A bloody big pair of woolly mittens," she answered.

CHAPTER 5

AIDS and the End of an Era

The headline almost leapt off the page at us from the Sunday morning paper, "*Aids to infect half the population within ten years.*" News of this terrible disease had been around for months and had made many people jumpy especially within the swinging scene, until then it was still perceived as a gay male disease and as such would not be a major threat to the heterosexual population. But now we were being told that it was spreading like wild fire among heterosexuals and the prophets of doom were forecasting a plague of biblical proportions, the tabloid hysteria had reached fever pitch and many expert doctors and professors were quoted as saying the disease was so contagious that you only had to be in the same room as someone and you could be infected.

Marie handed me the paper, she didn't speak, she didn't have to, I could see the worried look on her face. I quickly read the copy under the headline,

"It says here that people who have had sex with anyone other than their partner are at great risk" Marie looked even more worried.

"Shit," she whispered.

I continued to read, it didn't get any better. "It says the only chance of not contracting the disease during sex with an infected person is to wear a condom, and even that's only fifty percent effective." Marie slumped down onto the sofa next to me. Like the vast majority of swingers at that time, most of our sexual liaisons were unprotected. The few couples who insisted on wearing condoms rarely met anyone twice. It may seem incredibly fool hardy by today's standards, but back then, before the Aids virus became known, sexually transmitted diseases were easily treated by a swift course of antibiotics, and I can honestly say we never knew of anyone who had suffered anything more than a stubble rash, but Aids was a whole different ball game, it killed people, there was no known cure, and it was highly contagious, or so the media would have us believe. This was very bad news, if the papers were right and the virus could be caught just by touch we were in real trouble. Over the last seven years we'd had sex with hundreds of different couples, if just one of them had been infected, then the chances were we would have contracted the disease too.

"What are we going to do?" asked Marie.

"God knows," I answered. My mind was racing. If Marie and I really did have Aids, we could both die. What would happen to the kids? Christ, the kids could have it too.

The more I thought about it, the more I became convinced we must have contracted the disease. I began to panic, my heart was pounding and my mouth became so dry I could hardly swallow. The thought that we may have infected our own children because of our promiscuity made me sick to my stomach, I did my best to hide my anxiety from Marie but she was suffering too.

"We have to go to the doctors first thing tomorrow morning" she snapped. "We'll tell him everything; he'll know what to do."

"Just hold on," I said, desperately trying to inject a note of calmness into my voice, "Do you really want to go and see a man we've known for ten years and who thinks we are a normal everyday couple and tell him that we are really rampant swingers who, for the last seven years, have travelled the country screwing everyone between Lands End and John O'Groats?"

"What else can we do?" asked Marie, her voice just below panic level, I continued reading the newspaper.

"Well, it says here there is a test you can have if you have had unprotected sex in the last year and you think you may be at risk. You can go along to your local hospital and have a blood test, but they will only do it if you fall into a high risk category."

"I think we fall into that category ten times over, don't you?" said Marie, her voice now well above panic level. The following day was Monday and we spent a very restless Sunday night trying not to think of what news our visit to the hospital might bring.

Monday morning found us sitting in the G.U. unit at the local hospital, the waiting room was packed with people who had their faces hidden behind magazines and newspapers, the bloke opposite had his *Country Life* magazine upside down, and the young guy sitting next to Marie kept on patting his knees with the palm of his hands. I scanned the room. I didn't recognise anyone – anyone whose face I could see anyway. I had half expected the room to be full of swingers, a prospect I dreaded. I could imagine running into someone we had swung with a month or so ago. The conversation would have gone something like,

"Oh, hi, how are you keeping? Good session a while back eh? What are we doing here? Oh, we think we have Aids. Anyway, how are things with you?"

I shuddered at the prospect and buried my head in a motoring magazine, we had been given a ticket at reception with a number on it, I was number 17 and Marie 18. The room was overflowing now and the new arrivals had to stand around the edges of the room with their backs to the wall, nowhere to hide, I was thankful that at least Marie and I had arrived early enough to get a seat. Apart from the rustle of papers and the occasional nervous cough, the room was quiet, and sitting there in that atmosphere of doom and despair I felt a sense of shame, it was as though I had degraded myself, perhaps this was a kind of divine punishment for the life we were leading. I have always considered myself a Christian man. Don't get me wrong I'm no church goer but I have done my best to live by Christian values. If someone needed help I would do my best to help them if I could, I have never stolen anything (unless you count the little pens in Argos) I have never mugged old ladies or been unkind to animals, both Marie and I have strong family ties and believe the family unit is the foundation on which to bring up children. I have always worked from leaving school at fifteen to present day, and apart from one speeding fine and two parking tickets, I have never been in trouble with the police. So what celestial justice has decreed that I be sat here in this degrading waiting room with my wife who, like me, had led as good a life as she could. Is swinging so bad, are we so evil that we must be punished with such a hideous disease? As I sat there in my depressed state, I said a silent prayer.

"Please God, if Marie and I have to be punished, fair enough, but not the kids, please don't let them have to suffer, and if you can see your way clear God to just letting me have Aids and not Marie, the kids will need their mother you see, if you can please do that I would be eternally thankful, Amen."

This may seem morbid and even a little farcical now, but in my self imposed misery I had become convinced I had Aids and my last hope was that if God was listening to this I had to take my chance to be heard and at least save Marie and the kids.

The tannoy on the wall suddenly crackled into life.

"Ticket number one to consultation room one please."

There were three consultation rooms situated down a corridor that ran off to the waiting room, twenty minutes later my number was called. I gave Marie's hand a squeeze and walked down the corridor to door number three. Inside the small windowless room sitting at a desk, was a pimply faced young man wearing a white coat, he looked about sixteen.

"What can I do for you?" he asked abruptly without looking up.

"You can say hello, and ask me to sit down" I answered equally abruptly. I was in no mood to take shit from some young, spotty first year student who had drawn the short straw and had to see all the shame faced degenerates attending the G.U. clinic. I was wound up tighter than a drum and the anger and frustration I felt to say nothing of the shame of coming to a place like this had me ready to explode. He looked up clearly shocked by my answer.

"Please, take a seat," he said, nervously looking through some papers on his desk, "Now, what can I help you with?" His tone was much more personal now.

"I would like you to test me for Aids," I said.

"We don't do it routinely," he said "You need a reason to suspect that you may have been infected. For instance, have you had sexual relations with anyone not your current partner during the last six or seven months?"

"Yes," I answered.

"How many?" he asked.

"About two dozen. Maybe more," I said. Again he looked up, shocked.

"Two dozen!" he said.

"Maybe more" I answered.

"Were these men or women?" he asked.

"Oh, women, all women," I added quickly.

"Was this unprotected. I mean, did you wear a condom?"

"No," I answered.

He began scribbling in his notebook. "Have you had unprotected sex with your partner since?" he said.

"Yes."

He scribbled some more. "She will have to come in for a test in that case," he said, smugly thinking he had me back for my earlier outburst.

"She's here already," I said. "She's probably in the next room having it done now."

He put down his pen and looked at me quizzically. "So you've told her about the other women you've had sex with?" he asked.

"I didn't have to. She was there." I said matter of factly. His jaw dropped for a second, I could see he was desperately trying to work out what was going on.

"Did she have unprotected sex with any of these women?" he enquired.

"Some of them," I said, "But mostly she had sex with their husbands."

The pen fell from his fingers and onto the floor. As he fumbled to pick it up, I decided to put him out of his misery,

"We're swingers" I said.

"Sorry, I don't understand" he said.

"Swingers, you know, wife swappers." He just looked at me blankly. "We swap partners with other couples, for sex," I explained. His look of bewilderment seemed to be set in stone. "Have you never heard of wife swapping?" I asked.

"I thought it was just stories. I didn't think people really did it," he said.

"Well, now you know they do."

His eyes narrowed and he began to study me as if I would somehow look different to normal people. Perhaps I had little horns growing out of my head or an extra eye. His attitude had altered towards me. He now seemed eager for information. "How many couples would you swap with in a year?" he asked, his eyes still scrutinising me for abnormal features.

"Is that relevant?" I asked.

"Well, it could be, you see. If you prove positive we

would have to inform everyone you have had sex with for at least the last year, and then, of course, there are the people they have had sex with, and so on."

Now it was my turn to look bewildered. He was looking at thousands of couples if he wanted to track down everyone in the way he had suggested. My God, I was a one man epidemic. How could I possibly give the names and addresses of the couples we had met? That would be betraying their trust. But then, neither could I stand back and do nothing knowing they could be infected. This whole situation was getting worse by the minute.

"Just give me the test" I snapped. "Let's get it over with, then we'll discuss the who and how many."

"I'm afraid we won't have the results today" he announced.

"What? you must be joking!" I groaned.

"Afraid not," he continued, "It takes a week to ten days for the results to come through." My heart sank. I had psyched myself up for knowing the results now, not ten days time; this was turning into a complete nightmare.

I rolled up my sleeve and waited for the young intern to take my blood, he wasn't taking any chances, he put on rubber surgical gloves, a mask and a paper apron to do it. I felt like a leper.

"You'll get a letter in about 7 to10 days saying your test proved negative if you're okay," he said, after taking my blood.

"And what if I'm not?" I asked.

"We'll write to you and ask you to come back in for more tests" he answered softly.

Outside in the waiting room Marie was standing against the wall looking agitated.

"Where have you been?" she snapped.

"He wanted to know my life story," I answered ushering her out of the waiting room. Out in the car park we compared notes.

"I can't believe we have to wait over a week for the results" sighed Marie.

"What did you tell your doctor?" I asked.

"I said I was a prostitute and I had done it with a client unprotected," she answered.

"That's cheating!" I said, "I had to tell mine the truth. I'm still not sure if he believed me or not."

"Mine believed me alright."

"That's because you look like a tart," I laughed.

"Takes one to know one" said Marie. We were trying to joke but it fell pretty flat, we were both feeling low and I could not imaging how we were going to get through the next week or so. We both did our best not to touch the kids or even breath on them for the next few days, we became totally paranoid and soon found ourselves keeping our distance from family and friends, we had our own cups and plates which we kept separate and the girls bedtime stories were put on hold with the excuse I had a sore throat. I suppose we went into a kind of robotic state just doing what we had to do in a mechanical kind of way. We had convinced ourselves that we must be infected and the continued hype in the papers and on the television only served to confirm our certainty, it was a grim and miserable nine days.

The Wednesday morning post brought two white envelopes along with the usual junk mail. They were stamped and marked on the back with the local health authority logo. Marie got to them first but she was shaking too much so she handed them to me, I took a deep breath and tore open one end of the envelope, it had Marie's name at the top of the letter.

"It's yours," I said.

"Go on," said Marie, visibly shaking, I straightened out the letter and began to read. "I am pleased to inform you that your test for the H.I.V. virus has been returned as negative."

It seemed to take a few seconds to sink in and then she began to laugh and cry at the same time.

"Negative!" she shouted, "That means we haven't got Aids!"

"It means you haven't got Aids," I said.

"But yours must be negative too. If I'm okay, you must be okay. We did everything together."

"There's only one way to find out," I said, picking up the other letter. As I tore open the envelope my mind went back to the waiting room at the hospital and how I had asked God to spare Marie and the kids and just let me have Aids, if he had granted my wish I would have no complaints, just to know Marie was negative was a huge relief and as I pulled out the letter I felt a sense of calm I had resigned myself to my fate and accepted the inevitability of at least one of us having Aids.

My eyes shot straight to the second line of the letter. Negative. The word was there, no mistake. I was negative. I read it again just to make certain.

"I'm negative!" I gasped. Marie flung her arms around my neck; I closed my eyes and said another silent prayer of thanks. We stood in the hallway hugging each other for at least five minutes, neither of us wanted to lose this moment of utter relief, it was as though some monstrous burden had been lifted from our shoulders. We clung to each other so tightly that we seemed to merge, somehow becoming a single euphoric being, it was utter bliss and remains to this day one of my most cherished memories, strange how some of the best moments of your life seem to happen in the midst of adversity.

The Aids virus had a devastating effect on the swinging scene, a lifestyle that had been expanding steadily from the early seventies, now came to a grinding halt, the number of adverts in the contact magazines halved overnight, new couples once attracted by the excitement and adventurous lifestyle now preferred to keep swinging as a fantasy, and the few couples that still indulged, always insisted on using condoms.

That night we rang Danny and Sue, we had not called them for almost two weeks, we needed to be sure of our own situation before speaking to them, we had thought it a little strange that they had not rung us, the reason for this should have been obvious really but in our fog of misery we had not realised that they too had been for an Aids test, and as coincidence decreed had received their results that afternoon.

"Yeah, me and Sue are both negative," Danny boomed down the telephone, "But I don't mind telling you Baz, this last ten days have been the worst of our lives, so it has."

Thousands of swingers up and down the country must have gone through hell in that spring of 1987. Just like myself and Marie, Danny and Sue, had been caught up in the hysterical media reaction which was nearing its peak by the late summer of that year Aids we were told was so contagious that you could be infected just by being in the same room with someone who had the disease.

Eminent doctors and professors were wheeled out in front of the television cameras to tell us of the dire consequences of having unprotected sex, even petting and kissing were dangerous pastimes according to some stories. The scare mongering continued well into the autumn of '87, but things did not add up, we contacted dozens of couples who had in turn contacted dozens more and not one of these couples had heard of anyone with the Aids virus. Rachel, who along with Dave, had rushed to be tested like everyone else, confirmed that the private hospital where she worked had not treated any patients with the Aids virus or knew of any in the local N.H.S. hospitals. Slowly but surely the papers began taking a softer line, Aids was much less contagious than first feared and condom use gave almost total protection, the threatened plague which had been predicted as wiping out half the world's population was being amended to be only about thirty thousand worldwide. But the damage had been done, the swinging scene had gone stagnant, virtually no new couples were experimenting and many of the established swingers had decided to call a halt to their liberated lifestyle, for our part we decided that we would limit our liaisons to Danny, Sue, Rachel and Dave.

If all agreed, our intention was to form our own tight-knit group and not expose ourselves to outside contamination. As it turned out we included a couple called John and Julie who were special friends of Danny and Sue. We did not know this couple, but Danny assured us they were good people and could be trusted not to stray beyond the group, and as we were asking Danny and Sue to accept Dave and Rachel on our recommendation, it seemed only fair to take John and Julie on board too. We all met in a pub to formalise our agreement.

It was decided that night that we would only swing between ourselves until we all agreed differently we also resolved as an extra precaution, that we would use condoms. We had all taken the Aids test and proved negative, and as each of us passed around out letters from the hospital for the others to see, it felt cold and business like. None of us were comfortable with the situation, swinging had always been about spontaneity and freedom, it had been non conformist fun, a kind of unfettered emancipation, but now, here we sat, making rules and laying down conditions. It felt as though we had tarnished something beautiful, we all felt it, but it was the only way we could continue our lifestyle, and we settled for that. In truth, we had no other choice. And so the Christmas club was formed. We called ourselves this because it was so close to Christmas and our first decision was to hold a party where the eight of us could relax, have fun and get to know each other.

It had been almost two months since any of us had swung and this party would serve a dual purpose, first as a welcome chance to wind down, and secondly, as an icebreaker. We knew from experience that just because we get on with a couple, it doesn't mean to say others will. We didn't yet know if Danny and Sue would get on with Dave and Rachel or if we would get on with John and Julie, or Dave and Rachel with John and Julie, the permutations seemed endless and as we said our goodbyes that frosty night with White Christmas playing on the juke box, Danny gripped my arm and pulled me to one side "Baz my lad, promise me one thing, whatever happens we'll always be friends," I hugged him to me, "You can count on it Dan" I answered. He stepped back with that familiar grin spreading across his face, we didn't have to say anything else, we knew what each other was thinking. It had been a hard night and we both knew that hard times were coming. As Marie and I walked back to our car we passed a group of carol singers, they were singing Silent Night, we stood for a moment amongst a small crowd to listen. Silent Night, Holy Night, all is calm all is bright. We put some money into the collection box and made our way to the car. The carol was going around inside my head, the last few months had been horrendous, but now it seemed we had weathered the storm and all was calm again, but for how long. We would soon find out, the inaugural meeting of the Christmas club was just one week away.

CHAPTER 6

The Christmas Club

I was worried more about this first meeting of the Christmas club than any other group sex situation I had ever been involved in. Not because I was nervous of being with three other couples, we had done this many times before, but because of the people involved. Danny and Sue were our close long term friends, and Dave and Rachel had become almost as close, although we had only known them for a few months. My fear was that they would not hit it off and it would somehow affect our friendship with both of them. Marie and I felt responsible for them having a good time, we were piggy in the middle, and felt it our duty to make sure they all got on. It was a heavy burden to carry and had already knocked the edge off our excitement as the big day drew near. The other couple in the quartet were John and Julie, friends of Danny and Sue. We were to hold the inaugural get together of the Christmas club at Dave's and Rachel's house; it was the obvious choice as they were the only couple who did not have children at home. We had considered meeting at Dunromin, our hideaway rented flat, but it only had two rooms and would not adequately cater for eight people, so Dave and Rachel had kindly offered their home as the venue for our first assignation.

We had arranged to rendezvous with Danny and Sue and John and Julie just off the M1 at junction 31 and from there they would all follow us back to Dave's and Rachel's.

As we drove in convoy the few short miles to their home, I began to feel a deep foreboding of the nights outcome. I told myself that we were not responsible for everyone else and we could not be expected to nurse maid them through the evening, they were all big boys and girls and should take responsibility for their own good time, but by the time we had pulled up outside the steep line of steps leading up to Dave's and Rachel's front door, I was busy running through the myriad of differing scenarios the evening could bring and trying to formulate damage limitation plans should the worst case scenario actually happen. I should have been savouring the prospect of a hot steamy night of sex with four gorgeous women; instead my dark thoughts had only deepened my mood. As I locked the car door and led the way up the steps a light snow was falling out of the iron grey night sky. I noticed how the orange street light had cast a melancholy glow over our huddled group. We quietly climbed the steps; we were keeping the noise down so as not to alert the neighbours, but our self imposed silence only seemed to strengthen my doom laden expectations of the night ahead.

Dave opened the door as we reached the top of the steps, and ushered us in. Rachel came through from the lounge.

"Good heavens you all look frozen, take off your coats and come to the lounge to warm up." I was first through after Rachel, she turned for a second and gave me a nervous smile, I squeezed her hand. She had done her best to set the mood with subdued lighting and soft background music. Dave poured everyone a drink and then proposed a toast,

"To the Christmas Club, and long may it last."

"To the Christmas Club," we all echoed. I sat down next to Sue on the sofa, she immediately wrapped her arm around mine as if to confirm the fact that she had laid claim to me, Marie meanwhile had sat on Danny's knee, this left Dave and Rachel with Julie and John. I was concerned that Dave and Rachel did not think that we had chosen Danny and Sue over them, and yet if we had sat with Dave and Rachel first I would have been equally worried that Danny and Sue would have felt left out. This was turning into a nightmare and we hadn't even started yet.

The conversation flowed easily enough though, Dave and Danny both had their talking heads on and Danny's jokes had everyone in stitches. I noticed that Julie was really hammering the drinks, but I put it down to nervousness. John was coming on strong with Rachel, but if I was reading the signs correctly she was not showing the same enthusiasm for him, in fact she looked distinctly uneasy with his advances. I felt duty bound to help her out of her predicament, but how? Suzi Q was already nuzzling my neck and rubbing her hands over my crotch and the others had all slowed the conversation and were now moving on to kissing mode. Then it came to me, I had seen it done a few times before at parties when they had been slow to start, and it would free Rachel from John's clutches and level the playing field again.

"Hey I have a great idea" I shouted, everyone stopped what they were doing and looked at me, "Why don't the girls put on a show for us before we begin."

"What kind of show?" chimed Danny.

"A four girl lesbian show" I continued. No one spoke, they were still looking at me, trying to work out if it was a good idea or not. Marie had that puzzled expression she wore when she knew I was up to something but couldn't work out what it was. I pressed on.

"Rachel, do you have any baby oil?"

"Yes, in the bathroom" she answered.

"Great, you can oil each other up and the guys can dive in when we can't stand just watching any more." Danny, god bless him, fell for it hook line and sinker, "That sounds good to me Baz, so it does, especially the oiling up bit." With Danny on my side the others were beginning to come round.

"It could be fun at that. What do you say Rach?" asked Dave.

"I'm game if the other girls are," she answered.

Sue puffed out her cheeks. "Okay with me" she said. Marie, still looking puzzled, answered, "Why not?"

I looked over at Julie. "How about you, Julie? do you fancy a bit of all girl action?"

She downed another double vodka and stood up, almost falling sideways. "Just lead me to the fanny," she slurred, then let out a high pitched hysterical sounding laugh which ended in a loud hiccup.

"We'll take that as a yes," I said. The girls had a quick

chat and disappeared into the hallway to prepare the show. Julie grabbed half a bottle of vodka as she went, I saw John bury his head in his hands.

"Is Julie okay?" I asked.

"She's been drinking all day. She's been nervous as hell. I told her to go easy, but she just keeps knocking it back,"

"Does it make her aggressive?" asked Dave.

"Oh no, far from it," answered John, "In fact she's the life and soul of the party, but she doesn't know when to stop. If she has much more, she will be capable of anything, and I mean anything."

"Sounds like a fun girl to me," laughed Dave.

"Just wait until you see her perform, then you will see what I mean," said John shaking his head.

I wasn't unduly worried by Julie's drunken escapade and I felt a little easier knowing I had hopefully rescued Rachel from John's unwelcome advances, at least with the girls doing a show for us, it had thrown everyone back into the mixer and had given me time to work out a way to re-jig the pairing off. I was still taking it upon myself to make sure everyone was happy.

A couple of minutes later Rachel came in and spread a large pink bath towel on the floor of the living room, she then stood hands on hips and announced.

"Gentlemen, may I present the hottest show in town, this act has been banned in fourteen countries, but tonight, for your gratification, I present the members of the horny foursome, ready, steady, willing and able." As she spoke Marie walked in followed by Sue and Julie, we all cheered and whooped and hollered.

Danny shouted, "Which one is willing?"

"The whole fucking lot of them by the look of it" laughed Dave.

We all cheered and clapped as the girls began slow dancing and kissing each other. Now this was fun, and for the first time in the evening I began to relax. The four girls were now slowly undressing each other and rubbing themselves against each others increasingly naked bodies. Rachel and Sue knelt down on the towel whilst Marie and Julie stood behind them, Marie reached down and produced two bottles of baby oil, she passed one to Julie, who seemed to have legs of jelly, all the girls were now naked and Marie slowly poured baby oil over Rachel's shoulders. It ran down her cleavage, she caught it in her hands as it reached her stomach and proceeded to rub it provocatively over her body. Marie meanwhile had begun to rub the oil into Rachel's breasts.

This was horny stuff and all the men loved it. Julie now tried to copy Marie by pouring the baby oil over Sue's body, but she had not lifted the cap.

"It's not coming out," she groaned.

"Squeeze it," shouted Danny not knowing the cap was still on.

"I am squeezing it," answered Julie. Sue turned to see what was happening just as Julie with both hands gripping the bottle gave a mighty squeeze, the pressure blew off the cap and half the bottle of baby oil blasted Sue in the face as she fell back coughing and spluttering, she made a desperate grab for the towel and gave it an almighty tug sending Marie and Rachel flying sideways, a stream of baby oil from the bottle in Marie's hand arced through the air leaving an oily stripe across Dave and Danny's shirts and the arm of the velour sofa. Sue meanwhile was half hysterical as the oil had gone into her eyes and her vision was badly impaired. The lounge had turned from a place of relaxed sexy fun to a disaster area. We all looked bewildered at Julie who was still standing naked holding the half empty bottle of baby oil; she gave another high pitch giggle which again ended with a hiccup. We all turned to look at John, he had his head in his hands again, and slowly he turned towards Dave. "See what I mean?"

"I've never seen her like this" said Danny.

"That's because you've never seen her drunk" answered John.

Marie and Rachel helped Sue into the kitchen where warm soapy water was gently sponged over her face to wash away the baby oil. It would be over an hour before her vision improved sufficiently for her to feel comfortable again. John meanwhile, after apologising profusely to all concerned, had bundled Julie into an adjoining bedroom got her dressed and was ready to leave. It seemed hard on John, he was a nice enough bloke, and Julie was an attractive woman, but deep down I began to realise with them out of the equation, the night may work better, for one thing it had been obvious that there was no chemistry between Rachel and John, and Julie by virtue of getting paralytic had become a loose cannon. When men get drunk they can't perform and usually end up falling asleep, drunken women on the other hand can still have sex, but become unpredictable. I once made love to a drunken woman at a house party in Leeds and she suddenly started screaming that she was being raped, she was crying and shouting so loud the whole party came to a standstill. The husband finally appeared and began shaking her.

"She gets like this when she's had too much to drink," he said, "She'll be fine in a bit." He was right, within a few minutes she had stopped screaming and began crawling all over me again, but that was enough for me, women are a nightmare to understand at the best of times, but when they're drunk and sexy anything can happen. So John and Julie's departure had taken some of the pressure off me.

Sue eventually reappeared and sandwiched herself between me and Dave on the sofa. Rachel went and sat on Danny's knee, and Marie pulled Dave to his feet and led him over to the stereo.

"Now show me how to work this will you" she said softly. It was obvious the girls had taken control. I could feel the weight lifted from my shoulders. Sue felt good as she cuddled up to me.

"Make love to me Barry" she purred.

"Your wish is my command," I whispered. I could taste the baby oil on her lips as we kissed and her hair was still wet from the warm sponge. From her movements I could tell she wanted soft, gentle sex. The sofa was ours; it became our world, our bubble. I stroked back her hair and slid slowly down her body stopping en route at her breasts, belly and inner thighs before settling down to work gently on her vagina, slowly, softly I inserted my tongue and slid it from side to side, then top to bottom, coming back up I began to role my tongue around her clitoris. She arched her back and groaned, from my vantage point I could just about see through the dark pubic hair and over her mound of Venus to where Danny and Rachel were curled into an arm chair, they were deep kissing. Danny's hand was slowly and rhythmically caressing Rachel's breasts. Rachel's fingers feeling delicately for the buckle on Danny's belt. To their left by the stereo stood Marie and Dave, face to face, she was unbuttoning his shirt, his hands were resting on her hips, she was looking directly at him smiling that smile that left him in no doubt what she wanted.

Sue arched her back again, blocking my view, but I had seen enough to tell me that all was well now, and I could at last let nature take its course. The rest of the night melted into a collage of erotic moments, at one point in the evening we all found ourselves with our own partners, which we found hilarious, and by the end of the evening the six of us agreed that the inaugural meeting of the Christmas Club, although not having the best of starts, had been a resounding success, but we also agreed that it was not reasonable to expect the six of us to screw each other in perpetuity. If we had discovered one thing from the night it was that swinging is all about change and any attempt at maintaining a tight knit group at the expense of excluding all others, although probably fine for a short period of time, would eventually lead to stagnation and ruin. None of us wanted to lose or spoil what we had together, but we knew if we tried to keep it locked away we would eventually destroy it, like the song says, "If you love someone, set them free."

So the decision was made to meet others; in other words carry on swinging, the only proviso being we would agree never to have unprotected sex with anyone outside our group. Of course this was a matter of trust, almost a leap of faith. We had to be totally dedicated to this ethic, Aids would never go away, it had left a huge cloud hanging over the swinging scene and we all lived in the shadow of that cloud, and we all felt the chilling wind of change that it had brought, but we would not submit to it, could not submit to it, we fought back in the only way we knew how, by reasoned action and blind faith in ourselves and each other.

But a huge decision was looming for Marie and I; a decision we had felt coming for some time, and in its own way the Aids scare and subsequent diminishing and restrictive nature of the lifestyle had forced us to confront something we had been dreading. Now there was no escaping it, a decision had to be made.

CHAPTER 7

Time Out

As 1989 gave way to 1990 we welcomed the new decade in by making a momentous decision. We had decided to stop swinging. The beginning of the New Year served as a useful starting point for something we had been mulling over for the past few months.

It wasn't that we had gone off the lifestyle or fallen out with anyone, in fact we still had regular liaisons with out long term friends Danny and Sue and Dave and Rachel, and although it would be true to say we no longer got that electric buzz and the stomach churning excitement we experienced in the early years, we still enjoyed the scene immensely and although Aids concerned us, it was not a crucial factor in our decision. It was events and situations that had come about in our other life that had convinced us that swinging at least for the foreseeable future should no longer be a part of our lives.

One problem was our daughters. When they were children they were more than happy to stay with babysitters at the weekend, they had us to themselves all week, and most Sundays we would drive to the coast or some theme park and spend the day as a family, so our Saturday nights away had little impact on them but now they were both teenagers and it was becoming more and more difficult to explain our disappearances and sound convincing. Sixteen and seventeen year olds are the world's most inquisitive people, and remember this was seventeen years ago when the stigma surrounding swinging was only one notch above being a child molester or a rapist. We would have been mortified had our daughters discovered our secret, we knew of one couple it had happened to a few years earlier. Their three kids all in their late teens had disowned them and when the eldest daughter had a baby a year or two later she would not let her parents touch or handle the child for fear it may catch something from them. That scenario alone sent shivers down our spines and although we never considered for one moment that out own daughters could or would ever act in such a callous way, the fact that it had happened to someone we knew had a chilling effect on us.

Another reason for our decision was our shoe business, it had grown over the last six years to a point where the two of us working full time still found it difficult to cope, we had a shop, a small warehouse and two vans to maintain. Marie's younger brother helped out part-time driving one of the vans, fetching and delivering stock leaving me to look after the warehouse and wholesale side of the business and Marie to take care of the retail shop, it was hard work and long hours and even when we got home at night there were the stock sheets to go through and the books to maintain, so come the weekend we were becoming less and less inclined to get ready and drive fifty odd miles to meet people and go through the whole first meeting protocol. Even with our close friends where we did not need to go through all the polite conversation we still found on occasion that we would rather have settled down on the sofa with a hot cup of cocoa and watched television. It hit home to us one Saturday night when we found ourselves ringing Dave and Rachel with some flimsy excuse why we could not go over that night, as soon as we had made the phone call we knew we had done wrong and had some serious thinking to do.

These things weighed heavily on our minds and I had an added problem which affected me greatly in that new year of 1990 on the 22nd January I would be forty and I felt I should not be doing the things I was doing when I reached that age, it was a psychological problem I know, but still, it felt strange that I may on occasion find myself making love to a twenty one year old when I was forty I would be old enough to be her father, it began to bother me more and more as I went through my late thirties until now on my thirty ninth year it hung over me like the sword of Damocles. By today's standards forty is not old. I've heard it said that nowadays fifty is the new forty and that is true, but back in 1990 forty was the official beginning of middle age, much the same as fifty is today, and it was having a devastating effect on my mind. All these things had combined to bring us to our decision and so it was that the first of January 1990 brought an end to something that had been a huge part of our lives for the past ten years.

It wasn't what you would call a new experience for

us, after all we had been married for almost ten years before we began swinging, it was more of a return to the way we were, but with much trepidation. Could we just return to our pre-swinging days and be happy, or would the old quest for excitement and adventure overcome us again? It's true we were older and wiser now. We had seen and done more in the last ten years than most couples do in a lifetime. Would the fact that we had well and truly bought the tee shirt be enough to slake our thirst, or would the old longings rise to the surface again, only time would tell. One thing was certain, like the soldier who has fought too many battles, it was time to rest, to take a backward step and let the new generation take the lead. To say we were battle weary would not be strictly true, but we did need time to reflect on the last ten years to make sense of all the things we had seen and done.

Looking back I think that was the real driving force behind our decision to quit the scene, perhaps we needed to put things into focus and gain an unbiased perspective of the last ten years, kind of looking at the forest from a nearby hill instead of from the middle of the trees. Okay, no more analysing, I think you understand what I'm trying to say.

So began our second stint of monogamy. It was a life of details. A life of work, home and sleep. It wasn't as though we could spend more time with the kids, they were at an age when spending time with mum and dad was boring, pop music and boyfriends were far more important than days out with the oldies. We did book a family holiday to Majorca though which we thought would give us the opportunity to learn all about the latest boy band and new teenage fashions etc. It turned into a disaster. The first night there the two girls went off to the disco and missed their 11 o'clock curfew back at the hotel lobby. At half passed twelve they stumbled in more than slightly drunk and without a care in the world. Marie was in a panic and my remonstrations fell on deaf ears. We grounded them for two days, but Vickie, the eldest, stormed out anyway saying at seventeen she knew all about everything and could look after herself; sixteen year old Mandy locked herself in her bedroom and wouldn't talk to anybody for two days.

When we finally relented and let them both out together again the new twelve o'clock curfew was missed and Marie and I found ourselves scouring the bars and discos of Cala D'or. One thirty in the morning we found Mandy hugging a lamp post, "To stop it falling down," she said, and Vicky nearby chatting to a couple of Spanish waiters who looked like sure fire rapists to me. Anyhow that set the scene for the rest of the holiday, it was a nightmare, and Marie and I could not wait to get home. It was the last time either of the girls went away with us for many years until they had families of their own, when we became babysitters while they went out to enjoy themselves, talk about going full circle. But now back to the story. When we had made our decision to abandon our lifestyle we had called our closest friends Danny and Sue and Dave and Rachel to tell them the news. These were not phone calls we were looking forward to, but Danny and Sue were very understanding, they were the same age as us and their two sons were the same age as our own kids, so they could empathise with much of what we told them, and as Danny put it in the way only he could,

"Baz, just coz we're not shagging each other doesn't mean we can't be friends."

Sue was equally philosophical. "Everyone needs a break, maybe its time me and Danny took a bit of time out too." If they were upset they didn't show it, they wished us well and made us promise to have a drink with them soon.

Dave and Rachel were less understanding, they could not relate to any of the reasoning behind our decision. This came as no surprise to us as they had no kids at home and Rachel was six years younger than us with Dave being six years older, they both had well paid 9-5 jobs which gave them plenty of time to enjoy their lifestyle, the buzz was still strong for them. Try as we might we could not convince them that this is what we needed and was right for us at this time. Eventually they reluctantly gave up trying to talk us out of our decision, but told us in no uncertain terms that it would not last.

"Barry," Dave had said, "You're hooked. You can't escape. Nobody can. Once you've lived the lifestyle, you become part of it, and it becomes part of you. You may need a small break now and again but it always pulls you back."

Part of me knew Dave was right, we had seen other couples have time off from the scene, but they had all come back, perhaps we would too, we had set ourselves no time limit on our self imposed sabbatical, we were just going to run with it and see what happened. The truth is, we didn't understand ourselves all the intricacies of our decision, but we just knew it was something we had to do, call it instinct if you will.

Neither of us knew if it would last a week, a month,

a year or forever, we would rely on our instinct for that too.

In a strange way we had come full circle. Ten years ago we were taking our first tentative steps into the world of swinging and we were nervous as hell, now we were taking those same tentative steps back into the world we had left and guess what, we were nervous as hell again.

CHAPTER 8

Dream Boys and Lady Boys

We settled back into our daily routine easily enough. In reality the only day of the week that would change for us was Saturday, that's when the vast majority of our swinging sessions used to take place. So the rest of the week we did pretty much what we would do anyway. What was missing was the expectation, the slow building of excitement that comes when you know that come Saturday you will meet someone for sex, sometimes friends, sometimes strangers.

We found ourselves at first trying to compensate for our missed swinging sessions by substituting things like visits to the cinema or meals out in their place. But we soon realized that if we were going to live without swinging we would have to let our new lifestyle stand or fall on its own merits. So we stopped forcing ourselves to go out somewhere to stop us thinking about what we should normally be doing. We just stayed in, put our feet up and watched television.

It was strange at first; we kept looking at the clock and figuring out where we would be or what we would have been doing at a particular time. But as the weeks went by we did this less and less and eventually found ourselves in a sort of comfort zone where we actually looked forward to our nights in front of the telly, in bed by 11:30 and a long sleep in on Sunday mornings.

We didn't see much of the girls, like all teenagers they were either out or when in the house listening to their walkmans, or on the phone to friends. It really was just me and Marie on our own again. And we seemed to cling to each other emotionally.

We sensed that changes were all around us, some of it self-inflicted, some of it just a natural progression of children growing up and pulling away. We felt isolated and if truth be known, a little scared. In no time at all our daughters would be flying the nest and starting families of their own, they were already flexing their independence at every opportunity. We knew it was the way of things, but in our own selfish way we felt let down as though we had sacrificed a huge part of our lives to be at home on a Saturday night, so the least they could do was stay in and enjoy it with us. Of course it was never going to happen. The old ways were over and we would just have to get used to our kids not being children anymore.

It was traumatic in some ways to suddenly realise that they don't need or rely on you any more, they don't run to you for comfort if they graze their knee, they don't cuddle up next to you when watching a scary film or hold your hand when you cross the road, no more bedtime stories, no more rough and tumble on the back lawn, no more rushing home from school to show you a picture they had drawn or a biscuit they had baked, no more hugs and kisses.

I missed them as children, I wanted them to keep on

being children, but they were now young women with lives of their own to explore, and if they were to grow and expand their existence then we had to let them go. As much as we loved them and wanted to protect them we knew there was no alternative but to stand back and let them fly free. I think it's the moment every parent dreads, and it's the loneliest feeling in the world. Looking back I believe one of the main reasons we instinctively gave up swinging at that time was because we sensed that radical changes to our family structure were imminent and we needed to harness all our resources as a couple to deal with it.

I turned forty, the weeks grew into months and we threw ourselves into our work. We had to find our centre again, go back to the old ways, way back to before even the kids were born. We were like a moon thrown out of its orbit, the centre of our universe had shifted. If we were ever to find it again we would have to retrace our steps back to the beginning when it was just Marie and I, when we didn't have a care in the world, when we were just happy being together.

Every three or four weeks we would get a phone call from Dave and Rachel, just to see how we were surviving and if we were ready to swing again, but they didn't really push us, and most of the time we were happy to have a laugh and a joke with them. But we always refused their invitation for a drink because we had feared they would come on to us, and it could turn into an embarrassing situation if we refused.

Danny and Sue were less demanding. We met them occasionally for a drink and they always respected our decision, although I have to admit to being sorely tempted on one occasion when Sue gave me a peck on the cheek as they were leaving and I caught the fragrance of her perfume as she held my gaze for a second with those big brown eyes. But that apart we put swinging to the back of our minds and got on with our lives.

We had our first holiday together without the kids, it was strange, it was quiet. We missed the chatter, even missed their arguing. But we found in our solitude a strength, and a sense of satisfaction of having brought up two wonderful young women who would enhance the world and make it a better place.

By the time we returned from our two weeks in the sun we had come to terms with our new roll as standby parents and the more we acknowledged our situation the more we realized that there were fringe benefits to not being full time parents anymore. We didn't have to think of anyone but ourselves most of the time. No babysitters to arrange, no having to be back for a certain time to get the kids to bed. We had gained a freedom of sorts and in many ways life became easier.

Our transition from being doting parents to being just the two of us again had been a bumpy ride, but we were finally coming out the other side. We have spoken to many people over the years who have been through the turmoil of kids growing up and leaving home, some have welcomed their release of responsibility, but most felt, like us, abandoned, lost, and a little scared. I make no apologies for going on about this at length. It was a big event in our lives and as you will see later had a major effect on our future.

Towards the end of 1991 was Sue's birthday, the big 40, Danny's had been earlier in the year and we had all got together for a celebratory drink. Now it was Sue's turn and Danny, as usual, had laid on something special. "We had the family and friends party the other day," said Danny on the phone, "So there's going to be a bit more fun at this one." He had booked a room above a pub and would not tell us what he had planned, other than Sue was going to love it. We knew from experience that this was not always the case.

We arrived at the pub and were ushered up some stairs to the private party. There were maybe about fifty people in the room, most of them couples. We recognised lots of them, had had sex with lots of them. There was a half decent buffet spread across a couple of tables and the first drink was free. Danny had really pushed the boat out this time. We got chatting to a group of people we knew and I began to scan the room. There was still no sign of Danny or Sue. As I listened to the piped music blaring out some obscure song, I realised just how long it had been since we had been in the company of swingers. Their conversation was easy and open and sprinkled with words like "blow job," or "doggy style" and "quick fuck" terms that would cause offence in any other company. One lady in the group then produced a nicely rounded breast from her dress to show us all the slightly bruised nipple from her last encounter. Of course none of this was new to us, but it did bring home to us what a marginalized life we had been living since we had turned our backs on the lifestyle. We were amongst our own again and it felt good.

Suddenly Danny's thunderous voice boomed down a microphone, he stood on a small stage at the other end of the room fiddling with the mike, it whistled, it whined and then came to life.

"I would like to thank you all for coming here," he said in a hesitant voice.

"As you know, its Sue's birthday and I want it to be special, so I've arranged a little surprise."

"You've turned celibate!" someone shouted.

"If I had your dick, I would," Danny shot back, always quick with a response. A loud cheer went up. Danny continued,

"Right, Sue is in the next room, blindfolded, I'm going to bring her out soon and sit her on this chair and leave her in the capable hands of..." Danny paused for a moment as, from behind the curtain to his left, stepped three bronzed Adonis.

"The Dream Boys!" announced Danny. Another loud cheer filled the room as The Dream Boys went into a succession of body building poses. I could see every woman in the room licking their collective lips. If The Dream Boys thought this was going to be a normal gig they were very much mistaken.

Just then Danny spotted us at the back of the crowd and shouted down the mike.

"Baz my lad, glad you could make it. Where's Marie? Oh, there she is. Now Marie you're not going to get drunk and swing from the light fitting with your tits out and your knickers round your head like you did last year, are you?"

Marie turned a nice shade of red and forced a tight-lipped smile. "I'll kill him," she whispered. I could hardly hear her above the laughter.

"But you've got to admit, it was funny," I laughed, but Danny was not finished yet.

"And Baz, I've got those lady boy magazines you

ordered. I've put them under the bar, you can collect them later."

"Now, that was funny," shouted Marie above the catcalls and laughter. I gave Danny the thumbs up and mouthed 'good one' at him as his face creased into that mischievous grin.

I was relieved when they led Sue in blindfolded and sat her on a chair in the middle of the room. She sat there stoically, probably fearing the worst, but I could have told her that this was one of Danny's better birthday presents and one that she was sure to enjoy.

As the Dream Boys began their routine, I couldn't help thinking that these guys were in for a shock. They were probably thinking that Sue was going to be shocked or even shy and embarrassed by their antics. They didn't realise that there were women in this room who could eat them for breakfast without breaking sweat, and Sue was one of them. As they removed her blindfold and danced provocatively around her they were blissfully unaware what fate awaited them. They went through the old banana in the shorts routine, then the whipped cream on their nipples for Sue to lick off, then the warm baby oil for Sue to rub in. It all got too much for the rest of the women in the room and I could see them moving closer, tightening the circle. By the time The Dream Boys had realised what was happening, it was too late. A good twenty of the girls had surrounded them and were moving in for the kill. It was like Custer's last stand, and the girls certainly got their little big horn that night.

It was tremendous fun watching The Dream Boys being devoured, and although Marie took no part in it, I could see the sparkle in her eyes and the spring in her step as we joined in the cheers and applause as the last of The Dream Boys gave his all.

"I think they'll be known as 'The Cream Boys' from now on," she laughed.

"They've sure been creamed tonight," I said.

We went over to the buffet table and picked a few curled up ham and cheese sandwiches.

"Did you want to get involved?" I said to Marie, as she pulled the ham from the stale bread.

She cocked her head sideways. "I suppose I did," she answered, "Not so much for the sex but for the sheer hell of it," she paused again. "I miss the outrageousness, if that's the right word."

"It's as good a word as any." I answered. I knew what she meant. Tonight had been a revelation for us, our instinct was telling us it was time to get back into the front line. We had convalesced for almost two years and now it was time to join the fray again. We both sensed it and tomorrow we would ring Danny and Sue to tell them of our decision.

I gave up with the dry sandwiches and made do with a mini sausage roll. On the stage Danny and a couple of other people were involved in a condom over the head competition, and Sue was trying to bring one of The Dream Boys back from the dead by giving him the kiss of life. So we decided not to spoil their fun and slip away quietly. But as we neared the door Danny's voice boomed over the microphone one last time.

"Don't forget those lady boy mags Baz. They're under the bar in a brown paper bag."

CHAPTER 9

Ice Cubes in Edinburgh

Our old friend fate had intervened again to dictate our first swinging assignation after our time out from the scene. We had called Danny and Sue the morning after Sue's Dream Boy party only to be told by their eldest son Liam that Danny had taken Sue on holiday for two weeks.

Our next phone call to Dave and Rachel was equally unproductive, for although they were both overjoyed at the prospect of a much anticipated swinging session, they had both recently come down with the flu and would not be in a fit state to enjoy themselves with us or anyone else for weeks to come.

So we found ourselves in the strange predicament of being back on the scene but with no one to swing with. We had wanted our first session to be with people we knew and felt at ease with. Of course we could have held on for a few weeks for Danny and Sue to return from holiday, or waited for Dave and Rachel to recover from their flu, but we felt we needed to get involved again quickly. I think we feared that now the decision had been made we had to strike while the iron was hot, lest we fall back into the apathy we had just climbed out of.

We had lost a fair bit of confidence while we had been out of the scene and both put on a few pounds. We felt vulnerable again, maybe the lifestyle, as it was becoming known, had moved on without us, perhaps we would not be able to hack it any more, perhaps we would not fit in. We had to get back in the saddle and face our fears and doubts, any delay might force us to review our decision again.

Throughout our self imposed segregation we kept receiving letters from other couples sent by various swinging magazines. We would just write back that we were no longer in the scene. But occasionally a letter would stand out in our memory.

One such letter was from Angus and Zoe from Edinburgh, they seemed a fun couple who lived life to the full and we also liked the look of their photo. We had learned a long time ago that great looks and great personalities seldom go together. You mostly get one or the other.

Most of the time it's a trade off and you're happy to find either one of those traits in the people you meet. We only knew of two couples who had them both, so this letter from Scotland intrigued us.

Angus and Zoe were an attractive couple, even with Angus' huge ginger handlebar moustache which gave him a wing-commander look. Zoe had black hair, dark eyes and a dusky complexion. The beaming smiles they both wore were the clincher for us though, and their letter spoke of fun and laughter, and not taking life too seriously, that part really appealed to us. We had just been through a stressful period in our lives and the last thing we needed or wanted was to meet people who had a solemn outlook on life.

We called them on Monday and by the following Saturday we were heading up the Great North Road to Scotland. They had invited us to stay over, saying that there would possibly be two or three other couples there. It seemed they held these small get togethers every few weeks. That suited us fine; it would be less intense with others around.

We had never travelled this far before for a swinging session, but our new found enthusiasm kept us from questioning whether a four hour journey was the best way to begin our next swinging chapter.

Edinburgh is a magnificent city, we were impressed by its majesty and architecture then and it still remains one of our favourite places in the UK. We drove down the wide boulevards with their bright lights, modern shops and hotels and marvelled at the side roads that looked as though they had come from a Dickens novel with cobbled lanes and gaslights, they seemed like glimpses of the past, as if we were on some magical tour bus through time. The castle was the next thing to claim our attention; standing on top of a huge rocky outcrop it dominates the whole city, truly an impressive sight. The place is steeped in history and we were both captivated by the vibrant atmosphere, a mixture of old and new combining to produce an ambience we have never felt anywhere else. So much so, that by the time we found Angus and Zoe's address we felt elated and had forgotten our fatigue from the long journey.

They lived in what had once been part of the docklands but was now a trendy area filled with yuppie homes, bistros and chic restaurants. Pavement artists vied for position with the street theatre groups as throngs of American and Japanese tourists took photographs with their state-of-the-art cameras.

Angus and Zoe lived in what seemed to have been an old dockside warehouse, now lavishly restored and renovated to provide fashionable upmarket homes for the nouveau riche of Edinburgh. We took the lift to the top floor which was four storeys high and stepped out onto a long landing. There were only three doors, each one about thirty feet from the other.

"Wow, these pads must be huge," I whispered to Marie as we trod the thick maroon carpet to the end door.

"This is it, number 12C," I said, as I pushed the door bell and waited.

We could hear movement from inside. Footsteps, sounding far away at first but becoming steadily louder. After what seemed like an eternity but was probably about ten seconds the footsteps reached the other side of the door, a clatter of bolts and locks took another ten seconds and the door swung open.

Standing before us in all his finery, complete with kilt, dress-coat, sporran and socks was Angus, his huge ginger handlebar moustache seemed to take on a life of its own as he smiled widely and flung open his arms in greeting. He was a heavy-set man and his bear hug welcome almost crushed Marie.

"Come on in" he said in a broad Scottish accent, "Ye must both be shattered from the journey, come and have a wee drink."

As he ushered us in I could see why it had taken so long to answer the door, the room must have been fifty to sixty feet long and half that wide. Ornate original iron poles were spaced every fifteen or so feet holding up the roof, which must have been at least twenty feet high. The whole apartment, if you could call it that, was open plan with Chinese style paper panels dividing the various areas. The furnishings were modern with futons and scatter cushions in abundance. The living area was at the far end of the room.

"Zoe!" Angus called from the door, "It's Barry and Marie, all the way from Sheffield. Come and say hello!

From a huge brown sofa at the far end of the room I saw a figure rise and walk towards us, she seemed to almost glide across the parquet floor and met us halfway. Her photo had not done her justice; she was a very attractive woman with long black hair and dark green eyes. She was not tall; probably about five two but had a full hourglass figure. I began to feel the rush of excitement in the pit of my stomach, an experience I used to feel every time I met a woman I really fancied, and I really fancied Zoe.

After the initial greetings we retired to the big soft brown sofa and relaxed. Zoe told us the other couples would be arriving in a couple of hours so we had time to have a drink, shower and get ready for the night's frivolities. Angus handed me a glass of whiskey, it looked to be at least a treble.

"Here's a wee dram to clear the dust from your throat," he growled. I took a sip and then a gulp and gasped as the fiery liquid blazed a trail down my throat.

"That's strong stuff!" I wheezed. Angus nodded approvingly as I took another swallow.

"Aye, its extra strong, ye can'e buy it in the shops. I

get it from an old man in Portabello, has his own still." Angus tapped the side of his nose and winked before replenishing my glass, my protests fell on deaf ears.

"Nonsense laddie, ye must fortify yerself for the night ahead, you've had a long journey and need some fire in yer belly to keep the lassies happy." I drained the glass again and grimaced as long flaming tendrils of fire washed through my stomach and up through my arms.

"Now we really must go and shower" I said quickly, before Angus could fill my glass again. As I stood up I noticed a slight wavering motion that I didn't have when I had sat down.

Zoe led us through a door at the end of the lounge into a bedroom complete with a walk in shower and huge Victorian style bath. Fresh towels had been lovingly folded on a small shelf.

"Take as much time as you need," said Zoe, "The other couples won't be arriving for another two hours yet." Marie headed for the shower but I began to run the bath, I needed to relax and let the effects of Angus' extra strong whiskey subside. I began to feel better as I lay in the warm soapy water. I have never been a big drinker and the drinks Angus had given me had caused a warm glow inside, and now my head had stopped spinning I could appreciate the after taste. An hour and twenty minutes later we emerged into the living area again, freshly scrubbed and ready for action.

No sooner had I dropped down onto the sofa than Angus had thrust another tumbler into my hand.

"We've just time for a wee nip before the others arrive" he said.

"Well just a small one," I stammered, as Angus filled

my glass to the brim. When I tasted it I was amazed at the delicate flavour, I had expected the fiery trail of whiskey but this was something quite different.

"This is terrific," I said. A smile spread across Angus' face.

"It's my own elderflower wine," he said.

"I wouldn't have believed home brew could taste so good!" I said as I sipped, appreciatively, at the elderflower. I hadn't got more than half way down my glass before Angus was reaching inside his drinks cabinet again. This time he emerged with a bottle of dark red liquid.

"Try this," he said eagerly. I was beginning to feel like a professional wine taster, and rolled the first mouthful round my tongue with my eyes closed.

"It's fruity. There's something familiar about it. It's, it's..."

"Blackberry!" shouted Angus triumphantly, "Two years old this summer." I took another drink of the rich dark wine; I could almost see the heavy hanging clusters of berries, black and succulent, glistening in the autumn sun. The mellowness of the images matched my mood, which was becoming more genial by the minute.

"You know, Angus," I said holding the glass high and studying its ruby depths against the light, "I can't make out which one of your wines I like the best,"

"Ah, laddie," said Angus, clamping a hand on my shoulder, "We have ne even started yet, ah'v got dozens of bottles in there, all different. Ye must try a few more."

Just then the doorbell rang and Zoe shouted down from the other end of the room, where she had been showing Marie some sort of ornament.

"That will be the others. Pour some drinks will you, Angus."

"Your wish is my command," answered Angus as he disappeared into the drinks cabinet again.

I could see a group of people enter the room. I stood up swaying a little, but a slight blurring of the vision was soon shaken off by a quick rub from the back of my knuckles. As I walked towards the chattering group I could see Marie looking up at me intently. I had assumed that I had adopted a warm friendly smile, but I was told by Marie later that it was in fact a stupid grin. Nevertheless I got through the initial introductions without mishap and noted the two new couples were attractive and friendly.

In no time at all Angus had filled everyone's glass and I found myself back on the whiskey. It became obvious after a very short time that the new couples could drink whiskey like water. Not for them the slow sipping of the soft Englishman, no it was down in one followed by a facial contortion and then an expletive of satisfaction. Two whiskeys later and I was struggling so I retreated back to the elderflower wine. The others viewed me with a gentle benevolence, as though instinctively knowing I could not hope to keep up. For my part I had huge admiration for their stamina and all round fortitude, and as the night wore on a mutual respect was born between us.

The biggest difference between Scottish swinging parties and English swinging parties are that Scottish parties tend to involve huge quantities of drink, and the men and women for most part keep segregated until it's time for sex to begin, whereas in England the couples tend to integrate from the start, and don't consume so much alcohol.

There are pros and cons to both formats. The Scottish dos are much more social affairs with the guys having a laugh together before the action starts. The girls also seem to have a good laugh and a joke before getting down to business. There is much more social interaction at this kind of party. Whereas, the English parties are much more subdued affairs, with the onus on the sex and not on the social. We have been to quite a few parties in Scotland over the years and it's always the same, drink laugh, drink drink, laugh, shag. South of the border it's shag, shag, drink, shag, shag, drink (this last drink usually coffee). But this was our first experience of Scottish hospitality and after two hours we were still in the drink, drink, laugh stage.

Presently Angus rose to his feet, clutched at the table, and stood blinking for a few seconds.

"A toast!" he shouted.

"A toast!" we all echoed, and waited for Angus to speak. He stood swaying for what seemed like an eternity.

"A toast to what?" asked Stewie, one of the other guys.

Angus looked down blankly. "Ahv fucking forgot!" he cried as he slumped back into his chair roaring with drunken laughter.

We all cracked up, Stewie fell off his chair, Malc blasted a mouthful of whiskey over Angus as he exploded with laughter, and I just sat there howling and fighting for breath, trying not to spill what was left of my tenth glass of elderflower wine. That proved to be the catalyst for the real fun to begin as the girls wandered over from their own party to see what all the laughter was about.

It suddenly struck me that I had drunk too much. I had been having such a good time with the blokes, drinking, laughing and telling jokes, I had almost forgotten why we were here.

I was soon reminded when a cute little blond going by the name of Lisa came and sat on my knee. No sooner had she introduced herself than she began to French kiss me. Now it was obvious that Lisa had been on the sherry, remember I was now a professional taster, and I could detect the merest drop of alcohol, whether it be a fine malt whiskey or the delicate ambience of elderflower wine. And in Lisa's case it was definitely sherry, and by the way she was thrusting her tongue down my throat, another few minutes and I could have told you the year it was made, the brewer's name and his favourite colour.

Lisa pulled me to my feet and led me unsteadily to a bed-settee thingy called a futon. There must have been about five or six of these things spread around the place. Once there, she proceeded to undress me. I could see she was almost as drunk as I was which was great because when girls get drunk they tend not to want all the foreplay that most sober women love.

My fear was that I would not be able to perform, having consumed so much whiskey and wine. As it turned out I need not have worried, by the time Lisa had removed my boxers, I was standing to attention and ready for action. It had been almost two years since I had made love with another woman, and my excitement levels had overcome any desensitising effect the drink may have had. I think also the drink had helped conquer the anxiety and apprehension I felt coming so far from home on our first assignation after our lay-off. But whatever the reason, I was on top form and proceeded to give Lisa the shagging of her life, at least it seemed that way to me at the time.

The night carried on with more drinks, and more sex, no one was sober, and by three o'clock in the morning all that could be heard was the occasional snore. The room was warm and pieces of clothing were scattered all over the place. Everybody was naked, although I did notice that Angus still had his tartan socks on. People had fallen asleep where they fell amid half empty bottles and boxes of shortbread. I could see Marie curled up and sleeping like a baby a few feet away with a look of contentment on her face. I drifted off into a drunken sleep listening to the deep rumble of a ship's engine somewhere out in the bay.

I had no idea how long I had been asleep but it was still dark when I awoke to the sensation of someone playing with my dick. I forced my eyes to open, mainly to satisfy myself that it was not a bloke. My luck was in, it was Zoe, she was gently kneading my balls and caressing my flaccid dick. It felt good but I was spent.

"Zoe", I croaked, "I think you may be flogging a dead horse. I've been shagging all night, and for the last hour, before I fell asleep, I was cuming steam."

Zoe put her fingers to her lips.

"Shhhhh," she said, "Just lay back and enjoy it, there's a special surprise for you." I did as she said. Some of the others had woken up by this time and were watching quietly. The room was still bathed in darkness and only the rhythmic breathing of those still asleep broke the silence.

Zoe had taken me in her mouth and I was amazed to feel the beginnings of an erection as she worked her magic. I felt the stirring and began to groan softly.

She was now knelt between my legs, head down sucking my penis, both hands cradling my balls. I gripped the edge of the bed as the waves of pleasure began to sweep over me and bucked my hips involuntary, but Zoe did not pull off as I ejaculated into her mouth. That's when she did it, reached down for the ice cube and in one swift movement inserted it into my arse. It was timed to perfection and the effect it had on my climax was devastating. I think the only parts of my anatomy still touching the bed were my heels and the back of my head as my whole body arched upwards. Even today it's hard to describe the incredible intensity I felt at that moment. It seemed to last forever as all-consuming, surging torrents of ecstasy swept over me.

It was, and still is, the best cum I have ever had, comparable to the most momentous orgasms I have seen some women experience over the years.

When I had eventually descended into normality again, the people who were awake and watching began clapping and cheering as though showing their appreciation for an artist, and I suppose in a way Zoe was an artist that night.

The noise woke Angus who hadn't a clue what had just happened, but he staggered to his feet and lumbered over to our tiny group. He bent low steadying himself with a heavy hand on my shoulder as he spoke.

Footnote
Only the round ice cubes with the hole in the middle are suitable for this procedure.

"In my 'pinion this is the best night ever. What do you say Baz, ish it or ishn't it?"

"It ish, Angus!" I replied, "It bloody well ish."

Zoe and another woman went into the kitchen and eventually emerged with a tray full of coffees. It was like nectar to a Sassenach like me and I gulped the black liquid down as though my life depended on it.

The next time I woke up was to the sound of clinking glasses and early morning chatter as Zoe, Marie, and the two other girls were tidying up. Light was streaming in through the windows and the hum of traffic rose up from the street below. My head felt like it was ready to explode and I was shivering from the inside.

"Water, water!" I gasped. Angus suddenly appeared holding a bottle.

"Would you like some whiskey with that?" he said as Marie handed me a glass.

"No, oh please, god no, no more whiskey," I stammered.

"Nonsense," said Angus. "A hair of the dog is what you need." He proceeded to pour a good measure of whiskey into my life giving water. I drank it anyway. I was so dry my mouth felt like a sand pit.

"More water, I pleaded, but no whiskey, just water." Marie produced a second glass which I consumed quickly in case Angus came back to contaminate it with more whiskey.

We were driving home in the afternoon so I spent the next few hours laying on the futon with a damp towel round my head. None of the others had a hangover, not even Marie who had wisely stuck to champagne all night. I felt like a real softy being the only one who felt like death. But as Angus said, "Not to worry laddie. We do this every few weeks. Ye did well to survive as long as you did!" It was little consolation, we had a four hour drive back, and I could hardly open my eyes, let alone drive a car.

Luckily a couple of hours later I was feeling a little better, so we gingerly said our goodbyes. As we got into the car Angus handed me a bottle of his elderflower wine. "I know how much you like it," he grinned.

Zoe came to the side window, gave me a peck on the cheek and handed me an ice cube wrapped in tissue. "It's to rub against your forehead while you're driving, unless you can think of anywhere else to put it" she said smiling.

"Ice cubes in Edinburgh" I said, "Sounds like the chapter of a book to me." We waved goodbye to our new friends and as we made our way slowly out of that lovely old city, something told us we would be back, and we have been, many times. But the ice cube trick was a one-off; it only works if you are not expecting it, and for some reason whenever I'm in Edinburgh ice cubes always spring to mind.

CHAPTER 10

Anyone for Tennis?

In the weeks after our Scottish escapade our confidence had returned. We had met Danny and Sue and Dave and Rachel and had rekindled the old spark. We had also kicked back into the gym and lost the extra pounds we had both put on during our self-imposed exile.

The early nineties saw something of a rejuvenation in the swinging scene. The Aids scare, which had all but decimated the scene in the late eighties, had subsided and the vast majority of couples now used protection when swapping. More and younger couples were also becoming attracted to the lifestyle. The old Victorian attitudes that had dictated British morality for nearly a hundred years were being challenged. Little did we know at that time, but in a few short years we would be at the forefront of that challenge by being the first people to go on nationwide television to defend the swinging lifestyle through our club, La Chambre, but that's another story for another time. For now, we were just glad to be back amongst the fold and living life to the full again.

One Sunday night in June 1992 the phone rang, it was Dave, he sounded excited, he told me that the boss of the company he worked for was going away for two weeks, and had asked him and Rachel if they would stay in his house whilst he was away with his family, sort of house sitters, rather than it be empty.

"Sounds reasonable," I said, still not fully realising why Dave sounded so happy.

"Baz," he said excitedly, "The house has nine bedrooms, ten bathrooms, an indoor swimming pool, Jacuzzi, sauna, snooker table, and tennis courts at the back, and it's set in 17 acres and even has its own lake."

"Wow!" I said, "Now I understand why you sound so cheerful."

"But that's not all," continued Dave, "The boss says we can have friends over whenever we like, so we don't get bored." It finally clicked what Dave was telling me.

"You mean…?"

"Yes you and Marie can come over for the weekend. We'll have a fantastic time, we've got the run of the place."

"When?" I asked.

"Next week. Tell Marie to pack her swimsuit. On second thoughts forget the swimsuit …hold on someone's at the door. I'll ring later with the directions."

"Can't wait," I answered. "Give my love to Rachel," I said as I put down the phone.

This was great we had the complete use of a des-res for the weekend and it wouldn't cost us a penny. Dave rang again a few days later; he told us the house was just outside Hathersage which is a very picturesque village on the edge of the peak district national park. It's a quiet haven for lawyers, managing directors and the general well-to-do business population of Sheffield and Chesterfield.

The house itself stood atop a hill overlooking the

village, and although built in the local stone and made to look Elizabethan, it was only about six years old and had every conceivable gadget. Dave was busy playing with one as we drove up the long drive to the front of the house. Huge electric gates at the top of the drive parted as if by magic as we approached, and closed behind us as we pulled up outside the large double doors at the front of the house. I could see Dave's grinning face at the window. He gave me the thumbs up and pointed excitedly to the gates which were opening and closing like bees wings. The big double doors opened and Rachel came out to greet us.

"David, stop it with those doors, you'll break them," she shouted as she hugged Marie. "He's like a kid with a new toy, ever since we got here all he does is go round pressing things and switching things on and off" she said.

"Yeah, he's just a big daft kid" I said. "By the way, where is the switch for the gate, I've got to try it." Marie and Rachel just shrugged their shoulders and walked through the cavernous hallway, I watched them turn into what seemed an even more cavernous lounge.

"Now this is some rich man's pad," I thought to myself.

"Baz, I'm in here." I followed the sound of Dave's voice and found myself in a sort of library come study. Dave was standing at the far end near a window in front of a panel of switches and dials that looked like it belonged in the cockpit of a Jumbo.

Before I had time to speak Dave had pressed a switch and a drinks cabinet had emerged from the wall, another switch, and a television swivelled out from behind a mock bookcase.

"This place is fantastic!" said Dave. "I've been finding switches all afternoon. I haven't a clue what most of them do yet, but it's great switching something on and seeing what happens."

"The gates," I said, "Let me try the gates."

"Oh, that one's easy. Its this big grey one here," said Dave, pointing to a switch at the top of the board.

"Gimme, gimme" I said, as I pressed my thumb against the switch and held it there, there was a slight humming sound and the huge black and gold gates at the top of the drive began to open. I lifted my thumb off and they stopped, thumb down and off they went again.

"The power, the power!" I shouted, "It's great!" Dave nodded, his face alight with joyful appreciation.

"You can set it on automatic, but where's the fun in that?" he said. "I'm glad you're here, Baz, Rachel just doesn't understand the fascination all those gadgets hold for a bloke." I put a sympathetic hand on his shoulder.

"Dave, she's just a woman, how could she?"

He nodded, "You're right, they don't have the technical knowledge or the scientific understanding to appreciate the expertise needed to operate some of these systems, now let's go and press something else."

Marie and Rachel were sitting on one of the three massive sofa's in the main lounge sipping champagne when we found them. A huge bay window looked out over half an acre of manicured lawn and beyond, to the wild moorland overlooking the village of Hathersage nestling at the foot of the hope valley. Thin wisps of smoke rose from the old stone chimneys and hung, still in the summer air as the sun set behind a treeless mountain sending its last orange rays into the darkening sky.

"So this is how the other half live," I said, as Dave and I drank cool lager from the bottle.

"You ain't seen nothing yet" said Dave. Over the next half hour he and Rachel gave us the grand tour of the house, from the snooker room with its full size table, to the 40 foot long indoor swimming pool. The outside of the house was equally impressive with tennis courts, formal gardens and a lake complete with ducks; there were even a couple of peacocks roaming the grounds, truly impressive.

Rachel, as usual, had cooked a sumptuous meal and as we relaxed afterwards with a glass of wine on the back patio watching the stars in the clear summer sky I couldn't help but feel a little envious of such a lifestyle.

"What's he like, your boss?" I asked. Dave rolled his wine around in his glass and drank it.

"He's a decent enough bloke," he answered, as he topped up everyone's glass. "A bit of a workaholic really, always first in and last out. Despite having such a marvellous home, I don't think he spends much time here."

"What's his wife like?" asked Marie.

"Looks a bit hard-faced to me," said Dave. "But then that's probably why he's shagging his secretary."

"He's what?" I said, almost spilling my drink.

"Oh yes," continued Dave. "It's common knowledge in the company. He goes on so-called business trips every few weeks and everyone knows its just a ruse to spend time with his fancy piece."

"Why doesn't he divorce his wife if it's that bad?" asked Marie.

"What, and risk losing all of this in a divorce

settlement?" said Dave. "No chance."

"And would his pretty young secretary want to know him if he was broke?" said Rachel. "I don't think so."

"No," said Dave "It looks like he's stuck between the devil and the deep blue eyes of his twenty year old trophy girl."

"Well, I'll tell you one thing," I said. "Fifteen minutes ago I was feeling envious of his lifestyle, but I don't think any one of us would swap our lives for his."

"Here, here!" said Dave.

"A toast," said Rachel, raising her glass. "To honesty."

"And friendship," interrupted Marie.

"And good sex!" laughed Dave.

"To honesty, friendship and good sex!" We all echoed, as we raised our glasses and drank.

I sat back looking at the others and listening to their light-hearted banter. I felt good inside. Honesty, friendship and good sex. We had said it all in a single sentence. One follows the other, it's a natural progression and it doesn't get much better than this.

We swam naked in the heated indoor pool; we played naked snooker, if only Dave's boss had known what we had done with the snooker cues. We ran through the house like children playing naked hide and seek, the loser having to commit a forfeit for the finder. I discovered Rachel one time hiding in a large walk in wardrobe full of ladies shoes, there must have been hundreds of pairs. I made love to her there where she'd hidden amongst the stilettos, and open toed sandals, the high-heeled court shoes and leather thigh length boots. She said afterwards it was a dream come true she loves shoes and she loves sex, so where better to be ravished than a ladies shoe cupboard.

The night just seemed to get better and better, we discovered a giant Jacuzzi in one of the bedrooms and all jumped in, the jets of water must have had an arousing effect on the girls as they were soon kissing and touching each other, much to the delight of Dave and myself. It must have been well after midnight when we eventually decided to have a coffee break and catch our breath.

Down stairs in the kitchen the smell of percolating coffee was a joy as we sat around a heavy wooden table chatting idly. Dave had told us earlier about the woods to the rear of the house, "It's all the boss's land. A ten foot high wall surrounds the entire estate," and now, as we sipped our coffee, Dave came up with a new game. "I've got it. We'll play prison break."

"What's that?" asked Rachel.

"I don't know, I've just made it up," answered Dave, "But how about this for a scenario; Barry and I have held you and Marie prisoners in the house, but somehow you manage to break free."

"Is there sex involved in this game?" I asked.

"I'm coming to that," said Dave. "So you break free and escape into the woods."

"Where does the sex come in?" I said.

"Just hold your horses. Now, once in the woods you do your best to evade capture from the pursuing guards."

"You and Barry," said Marie.

"Correct," answered Dave.

"What about the sex?" I said

"Once the guards catch you, the penalty for escaping is..."

"SEX!" I shouted.

"You've got it." said Dave.

"I like the sound of this game," I said.

Dave drained his coffee cup and threw open the kitchen door.

"We'll give you a two minute head start and, remember, when we catch you, you'll be in for a damn good rogering!"

"But we're naked!" protested Rachel.

"The clock's ticking," said Dave, tapping his watch. Marie and Rachel looked at each other and ran squealing out the kitchen door, we watched as they skirted the tennis courts and disappeared into the woods beyond, Dave counted out a minute and said, "Fuck it, let's go!"

We traced their route around the tennis courts and into the tree line. The moon was bright and cast a silver light on the trees, long black shadows lay everywhere giving sharp contrast to the moonlight. The wood was relatively open with trees widely spaced making it hard for the girls to hide. "Give yourselves up and we'll go easy on you" shouted Dave. A giggle from a clump of trees about forty feet to our left made us turn in that direction. Dave crept towards it while I skirted round hoping to catch whoever it was from behind. Apart from the crickets and the odd hoot of a night owl the woods were silent, only the crack of a twig or the crunch of bracken underfoot could be heard as we crept around. I had lost sight of Dave and listened intently for any movement, all was quiet, then all hell broke loose, it was Dave.

"I've got one!" he shouted, "It's Marie."

I heard Marie squeal as she darted from behind a tree.

Dave was after her like a shot. I could hear them shouting and laughing as they disappeared further into the woods. Rachel could not be far away, I stood watching and listening for any movement.

"Come out, come out, wherever you are!" Still not a sound. I moved stealthily around a large tree trunk and there she stood ghost like, her white skin shining like porcelain in the moonlight. She screamed, I screamed and she set off like a whippet. I chased her through a cluster of trees twisting and turning as we ran, she was much more nimble than I was and managed to gain a few yards but then we came to a small clearing and I caught up rapidly managing to bring her down on a soft mossy bank on the other side of the glade. I rolled Rachel over on to her back and held her wrists above her head, she was fighting me struggling to break free but I held her down, her auburn hair was strewn across her face from the struggle and her teeth flashed white as she thrashed her head from side to side.

"No one escapes from my prison!" I said, as menacingly as I could.

"What are you going to do to me?" she whimpered, still playing the part of the escapee.

"I'm going to teach you a lesson you will never forget," I said. I reached down and pulled up a huge clump of moss and began to rub it into Rachel's breasts, it was soft and damp with earth still attached to the roots and I smeared it all over her body. Three times as I sat astride her I reached down for more and rubbed it into her belly, breasts and over her pubic area. She was pleading for me to stop

"No sir, please sir, I won't try to escape again, what

are you going to do to me sir?" Rachel was really into the part and loving every second. I threw the last dregs of moss to one side and gripped her arms above her head again.

She gasped. "Ooohhh, no sir, not that, please!"

I clamped a moss stained hand over her mouth and told her to be quiet, then entered her and thrust into her again and again as she struggled to break free. On and on I went just thinking of my own pleasure, ignoring her pleas, until finally I climaxed inside her and relaxed my grip; breathing heavily I rolled off her and lay there panting. Rachel was panting too; she lay on her back covered in moss and earth staring into the night sky.

Suddenly a terrifying thought swept over me, what if Rachel's struggles had been for real, what if I had really forced myself on her, perhaps I had played the part of the evil guard too well, I sat up sharply.

"Rach, are you ok?" I stammered. "I feel like I've just raped you. Tell me you were playing the part, tell me you enjoyed it, please." Still breathing heavily, she turned her head. I could see the smears of moss and dirt on her face and body, beads of sweat sparkled on her forehead as she turned to face me.

"You brutal bastard!" she gasped. "You were like an animal, just using me for your own pleasure." She paused and took a deep breath. "It was the best damn sex I've had in ages!"

We caught up with Dave and Marie on the edge of the woods. When Marie saw Rachel she said, "Camouflage, now why didn't I think of that?"

"Not exactly," replied Rachel. "I'll tell you later." We were all laughing and joking as we crossed the manicured lawn to the tennis courts. About half way across we heard a loud clunk followed by two more as three massive security lights came on. They flooded the whole rear of the building including the tennis courts; it was almost like daylight they were so bright.

"Bloody hell!" exclaimed Dave "We must have triggered them when we crossed the lawn."

"Hey, we can have a game of night tennis" I said,

"Why not?" said Dave. We quickly found some rackets and tennis balls in a metal bin by the side of one of the courts and for the next half hour we enjoyed the delights of naked tennis. When we finally made our way to the kitchen for much needed refreshments, we had worked up quite a sweat, watching the girls boobs bounce around had been enormous fun to say nothing of the laugh they had watching our bits flop about, and hearing Dave's impersonation of John McEnroe (you cannot be serious) had us in hysterics.

The coffee pot beckoned in the kitchen, but no sooner had we got in than the phone began to ring in the lounge, Dave looked concerned, "Who can that be at this time"? he asked.

I glanced at the clock on the wall, it was 2.30 in the morning. "You'd better see who it is mate" I said, "it could be important."

Dave hurried through to the lounge, while Rachel poured the coffee. After a few minutes Dave came back in looking flushed

"Who was it?" asked a worried looking Rachel. Dave sat down at the table and took hold of his coffee.

"It was a security firm. My boss has hired them to monitor the outside of the house, it seems when the security lights are triggered they look at the cameras they have outside, to check for prowlers and intruders." We sat there dumbfounded.

"You mean they've been watching us play naked tennis for the last half hour?" said Marie.

"Yes," said Dave. "Seems they knew we were here because the boss told them, and usually when the light is triggered it's just a fox or a badger or something, but this time…"

Rachel interrupted. "This time it was four naked people playing tennis."

Dave nodded. "How many of them saw us?" I asked, holding my head in my hands.

"All of them, dozens" said Dave. "All the controllers came to watch, they said it was the best laugh they've had in ages." Marie and Rachel both groaned with embarrassment.

"They said the lights were so bright, spy satellites could have seen us from space." We all gave a collective groan this time. "There's more," said Dave.

"No, for God's sake, no more!" I pleaded.

"You remember, Baz, in the second set when Marie sent over that wicked back swing and you fell over trying to save the point?"

"Yes?" I said, cringing at the thought.

"Well they had a long discussion and even played it back a few times and finally all agreed. Both balls were definitely out.

CHAPTER 11

The Longshanks Monster

The name of Andy Longshanks had cropped up numerous times over the last few months; we had heard it mentioned at swingers' parties up and down the country. It seems Mr. Longshanks was becoming something of a celebrity on the scene due to the size of his dick, which varied in length – between ten and fifteen inches, depending on who was telling the story. Of course this meant that he was very popular with the ladies and had a great novelty value at parties.

Although we had heard tales of his exploits many times we had never actually met him, so when we heard on the swingers' grapevine that he was to attend a party in Leicester, we vowed to go along and see what all the fuss was about. After angling an invite, we were disappointed when Marie came down with food poisoning on the night of the party, but luck was with us. When I rang with our apologies and mentioned to the host that Marie had been looking forward to meeting the legendary Andy Longshanks, he called him to the phone and, after a brief conversation I obtained his phone number along with an offer to ring him sometime. This managed to bring a smile to Marie's face in between bouts of vomiting.

A couple of days later Marie was on the phone to Sue telling her with pride that we had the private number of Longshanks himself. Of course it was not long before Marie and Sue had cooked up a plan. This involved us getting together with Sue and Danny and inviting Mr. Longshanks as a single guy. Danny and I knew what the girls were up to, they just wanted to see and experience his giant appendage for themselves and we would be largely redundant on the night. But if the truth be known, we were as intrigued as they were to see if the stories were true and it might be fun to see if the great man could service these two incredibly horny females, so we went along with their plan. I duly rang Mr. Longshanks and made arrangements to meet up at Dunromin, our secret flat, the following week.

Now its not something one would put in their resume but I had become something of an expert on both male and female genitalia. As any full on swinger will tell you, the one thing you see plenty of in the scene is nudity, and over the years I had seen thousands of examples of both sexes in their birthday suits, not that I was a connoisseur or anything you understand, but you can't see something as often as I did and not become knowledgeable on the subject. The main thing to appreciate with human genitalia is its diversity; like fingerprints, no two are the same – you get long thin dicks and short fat dicks, some bend to the left, some to the right, some have big bulbous heads, some hardly have heads at all, some blokes are hung like donkeys when they are in the flaccid state, but don't get much bigger when they are hard, while some guys are really tiny when soft yet grow out of all proportion when aroused – hence the phrase growers and showers.

Women are no different. Vaginas come in a variety of different shapes and sizes, from the clean cut slit to the multi layered skin variety, and the length of the labia can vary enormously too. I've seen women with fanny flaps five inches long on either side, and some are so tight you can barely insert your dick. A few are so big you can push your fist in. I remember one woman on the scene in the early nineties whose fanny was so huge she acquired the unflattering nick name of cavern cunt. I never met her myself, but Danny once told me he'd had her at a house party and could not feel the sides, so he'd put his hand in to toss himself off.

"It's as true as I'm standing here talking to you Baz," he had said. He was sitting down at the time.

Anyhow the point I'm making is, the one thing you can rely on with sexual organs, is they are all different. That said, it is important to also realize that the vast majority do fit into a kind of framework, and this framework, with its wide parameters, accounts for 99 per cent of all subjects. But every now and again, someone would come along who was so far outside the framework as to be considered special.

Andy Longshanks was one such person. We had all seen guys with big dicks – they would usually be the first to take their clothes off at parties... they would walk around looking cool with their pride and joy swaying in the wind. They were known as showers, but I can't honestly say that I had ever seen anything when stood to attention much more than nine or ten inches, and that is really going some. The vast majority of men are in my experience somewhere between five and seven inches when erect.

So with an almost tangible anticipation, we awaited the arrival of our renowned guest. A knock on the door sent Sue and Marie scurrying across the room, Danny and I exchanged surprised looks and shook our heads.

"They're like star struck teenagers" I said.

"More like cock struck if you ask me" replied Danny. At that moment Sue and Marie entered the room, sandwiched between them was the great man himself.

Now I'm not quite sure what we had expected, perhaps some muscular Adonis with a shiny white smile or maybe a swarthy moustached ladies man with a twinkle in his eye, at the very least a tall good looking guy who would radiate an air of confidence. What we got was a thin, pale, sunken chested bloke with a big nose and buck teeth. He smiled nervously and held out a bony hand.

"Hi, I'm Andy" he said in a soft shaky voice. Danny strode forward and grabbed his hand.

"You're the bloke with the big knob" he bellowed – never one to stand on ceremony was Danny. I could see our guest was taken aback by Danny's less than tactful greeting, so wrestling his hand from Danny's vice like grip I introduced myself.

"Hi, good to meet you at last. This is my friend Daniel, and I gather you've already met the girls."

"Yes," he said smiling, "They've been very accommodating." The two girls had linked their arms into his and both wore beaming smiles, his lack of physique and looks had obviously not fazed them, their minds were focused on one thing and nothing would detract them from their quest. They were on a mission and I couldn't help but liken his predicament to a zebra between two lionesses.

Danny poured the wine as the girls eyed their prey. The conversation was superficial but mandatory; it would have been bad manners for the girls to devour our guest before the social niceties had been completed. It came as no surprise to learn that Longshanks was not his real name, it had been bestowed on him by one of the very first ladies he had serviced and it had stuck. Although he was a shy, nervous sort he was also unassuming and had a very personable demeanour which I suspected would endear him to most people. More wine was poured and the girls were prowling for the kill. Marie gave me a nod and I dimmed the lights while Danny put on some soul music, Sue and Marie pulled Andy to his feet and lead him over to one of the bed settees which had been opened, Danny and I went over to the other one and with a couple of cool lagers in our hands sat down to watch the show.

The two lionesses, sorry, girls, slowly circled their prey, never taking their eyes from his, occasionally letting a hand slide across his body as they moved around him. Andy held their gaze one to another his head spinning, waiting for them to move in, he knew it was coming but he did not know when. Sue began to unbutton his shirt, slowly seductively, she squeezed each button out of its captivity, her face was inches from his as she darted out her tongue to tease him.

Andy's eyes widened and he began to breath open

mouthed, his shirt was now wide open and Sue slid her hands inside and dragged her nails softly down his chest as he involuntarily arched his back, Marie equally softly clawed his buttocks, he stood rigid now, eyes closed, excepting his fate and loving every second. The girls began rubbing their hands all over his chest and back, his shirt lay on the floor, his thin arms thrust out long and straight either side of him as their hands roamed over his body, they unbuckled his belt being careful not to wander below just yet, preserving the moment, building the atmosphere and heightening the sexual tension.

At that moment Danny, who had been sitting patiently sipping his lager and waiting for the girls to move in for the kill, bellowed, "Come on, get on with it! Get his cock out!"

Both Sue and Marie shot him a withering stare. Andy Longshanks seemed to snap out of his trance and I had to stifle a laugh, the girls fearsome glare had forced Danny to retreat behind his lager bottle.

"Fuck me, Baz. All I said was hurry up, and see the looks I'm getting! Is there blood coming out of my ears?"

"I think they're working up to it Dan" I whispered,

"Well they want to hurry up, I've got an appointment at the dentist next Tuesday!"

The girls had resumed toying with their victim, but Danny's outburst seemed to have had an effect because they were finally getting down to business and unbuttoning his fly. That done they pushed him backwards onto the bed and, each taking hold of a trouser leg, pulled them off. Now as I said earlier, in all the time we had been swinging I had seen literally thousands of dicks, but here was Andy Longshanks in all his glory and it was obvious that he was special. He was only semi-erect but he was already well over the nine inch benchmark and it wasn't one of those long thin cocks either, it had girth as well as length. Marie and Sue both stood back in awe and appreciation, cooing at the prospect of getting to grips with this monster. A bottle of baby oil magically appeared and was poured liberally over Andy's giant appendage. As both girls began to massage the oil in, it began to grow and grow, Danny laughingly slapped his knee and shouted, "Don't let it wrap itself around you Sue. It's a constrictor, ha ha."

This time the girls took no notice. They seemed memorised by this still growing colossus.

Andy's sunken chest and bony hips and the complete lack of any body fat only served to make his dick look even bigger, but even given his slight frame extenuating the size, there was no getting away from it, this was easily the biggest cock I had ever seen. With the girls caressing and fondling him he now stood at his peak and I estimated it to be at least thirteen possibly even fourteen inches, a true leviathan.

Danny was equally impressed. "Credit where credit's due, Baz," he said. "He may be a skinny little cunt, but that's a cock and a half if ever I saw one."

One of the girls had produced a condom but it barely came half way down Andy's massive organ. We watched in awe as Marie gripped the bottom of the condom to stop it riding up as Sue impaled herself on Andy's cock. Slowly she sank down the shaft, eyes wide and mouth open until she could go down no further, there was still about five inches showing at the base of Andy's dick. Sue gave a guttural gasp as she bottomed out and slowly lifted herself up again almost to the tip and then lowered herself all the way down again. This she did six or seven times before gaining the confidence to increase her speed. Marie meanwhile, having lost her hold on the condom, was stood in front of Sue gripping her arms and helping her control her movements. Danny was wide eyed with disbelief.

"Fuck me, it looks like she's shagging a fence post!" he exclaimed. Sue's head was thrown back in ecstasy as she climaxed and Marie had to steady her and hold her up as her legs gave out and she rolled sideways, sliding off Andy's gleaming shaft. The condom came off with her and hung half out of her pussy like a deflated parachute. Marie looked down at the still panting Sue and asked, "Well, what did it feel like"?

Sue looked up and answered breathlessly, "It was like being shagged by a Shire horse" she then fell backwards onto the bed with a huge smile on her face.

Danny stood up and walked over to Sue, he put his hands on his hips and did his best to look indignant.

"So you've been shagging Shire horses behind my back have you, eh?"

Sue's smile got wider. "Yes I have to admit it," she answered. "But it was only the once and it didn't mean anything."

"Who was it?" Danny demanded, still holding a straight face. "No, don't tell me, let me guess. It's that Snowflake isn't it? With his big furry feet and white mane, it's him isn't it?"

"No it's not" Sue responded. "If you must know it's Dobbin. And there's something else – we're engaged!"

"Dobbin!" shouted Danny. "That overgrown donkey! How could you do this to me? Not Dobbin! At least Snowflake has his own teeth!" Marie, Andy and I were falling about laughing. When Danny and Sue went into one of their little comedy routines it was always hilarious, Danny was biting his knuckles in mock anguish.

"Can you believe it, Baz. She's been cheating on me with Dobbin, what does she see in him"?

"Could it be the size of his dick?" I said.

"That's it, Baz. It must be. It can't be anything else. I'm better looking than he is, I have a better personality, and I don't shit where I sleep." He rounded on Sue. "Dobbin might have a big dick, but can he do this?" Danny seized the end of the condom still dangling out of Sue's pussy and pulled, Sue involuntarily clenched up and the condom stretched to about two feet long, suddenly it exploded out of Sue and streaked like a missile across the room, eventually hitting the window where it stuck for a few seconds before sliding slowly down the glass, it was the funniest thing I had ever seen and, within seconds, the four of us were laughing hysterically.

Andy was laughing so hard he fell sideways off the bed and landed heavily on his elbow, his scream of pain and seeing him on the floor only made us laugh harder. Even Andy was still laughing whilst holding his injured arm, Danny was in hysterics, his face was crimson, tears streamed down his cheeks, his mouth was open but no sound was coming out, he just kept pointing to Sue's pussy and then to the window, and then to Andy who was still on the floor clutching his arm and laughing uncontrollably. I had to pound Danny's back to make him take a breath, otherwise I'm certain he would have passed out. Marie and Sue were just as helpless, and I had slumped down onto a chair exhausted, my sides aching from the laughter. It was contagious. Just when it seemed we had laughed ourselves out, someone would burst out laughing and we would all start again. It was a good twenty minutes before we all lay drained and depleted on the floor, the girls made a makeshift sling out of a bed sheet for Andy's injured arm, while Danny and I made a fresh cup of coffee.

The sexually charged atmosphere which the girls had worked so hard to create had gone, that and the fact that Andy's arm was giving him real pain meant that there would be no further sexual activity that night, so Marie did not have the pleasure of the legendary Longshanks monster on this occasion. She did make up for it a few years later though when we unexpectedly ran into him again, and what a session that was, but that's another story. Andy rang us the following day to say that he had cracked a bone in his elbow, but he'd had the most fun ever and, even though his elbow was giving him gyp, he found himself still laughing out loud occasionally.

"It's very embarrassing in company and its not like you can tell people what you're laughing at either." he added.

Marie rang Danny to berate him for ruining her pleasure. Danny answered, "But Marie darlin', can I help it if Sue has a missile silo for a fanny."

We met up with Danny and Sue a week or so later and Marie was still teasing him.

"Well, I suppose if I can't have a fourteen inch cock, I'll have to make do with four inches from you, won't I Danny?" she joked.

"Oh begorra," he answered. "That means I'm going to have to fuck you twice."

CHAPTER 12

The Flying Femidom

The A57, more commonly known as the snake pass, twists and turns its way over the rugged Pennine hills from Sheffield in the east to Manchester in the west, its not a trip to be taken lightly, landslides regularly block the road and sheer drops of hundreds of feet are only inches away from the roads edge for much of the way. In winter huge snow drifts make the road impassable for weeks on end and in summer pot holes appear out of nowhere as the tarmac cracks and falls away, all in all not the kind of road to embark on unless you have a very good reason. Our reason, as ever, was sex.

Our destination was Glossop, nestling at the foot of the giant Bleaklow Hill on the Manchester side of the Pennines, it was a grey granite mill town that seemed to be stuck in the nineteen fifties. Marie studied the A to Z as I slowly drove down the main road past the grey granite town hall, and the grey granite market square with its cobbled stones and rickety wooded market stalls, on past row after row of grey granite terraced houses.

"This is it," she said, "Turn left here. There it is, the one with the net curtains."

"They all have net curtains," I said.

"Number 36. Just pull up!" snapped Marie as she slid the A to Z into the glove compartment.

As we sat there straightening our clothes and composing ourselves we noticed the next door curtains twitching, and a face appearing at the window across the road.

"Don't look now, but I think we're being watched," I said.

"I know," answered Marie. "I think its one of those streets where you sneeze and everyone knows about it."

"Let's hope she's not a screamer then" I laughed. Marie smiled and shook her head, we had been to places like this before where the neighbours were so nosey they would stare at you openly from windows and doorsteps almost demanding an explanation as to why you were there. At least this street was a little more discreet apart from the woman across the road, it was mainly curtain twitchers.

We knocked on the door keenly aware that there must have been at least a dozen pairs of eyes on us, the door opened and we scurried inside hardly waiting for an invitation. We found ourselves in a small dark hallway, the front door had been quickly closed behind us taking with it most of the natural light, we strained to see who had let us in. We only realized it was a man when he spoke.

"Nosey parkers. Always want to know your business on this road," said the gruff voice. "Come through to the lounge." We followed him into a small living room. It was only marginally lighter in there, due to the fact that there must have been at least three layers of net curtains covering the window which fronted directly onto the street outside.

Gruff Voice went over to the window and parted the nets by about an inch, his eyes darting from side to side as he spoke. "Look at 'em still looking. They make you sick."

In an arm chair next to the window sat our hostess. She smiled but said nothing, as Gruff Voice pulled himself away from the curtains and went to stand by her side, where they both proceeded to just stare at us, this went on for about ten seconds, although it felt like ten minutes. Fuck me, I thought. We've got a right pair here. They're as bad as the bloody neighbours.

Now, when you go to someone else's home to swing for the first time it's usually incumbent on them to set the scene, make the other couple comfortable and generally make the running, but these two didn't have a clue. They either didn't get many visitors or had never learned the social graces. It was obvious we were going to have to take over. I thrust out my hand. "Tom and Lyn I presume?" I said, "Good to meet you both."

Tom nervously shook my hand. "You're Barry and Marie," he said.

"That's right," said Marie. "He's Barry and I'm Marie, in case you were wondering."

Tom and Lyn looked puzzled – not quite sure if Marie had made a joke or not. It was going to be a long night.

Over the course of the next hour we managed to extract enough information from them for us to ascertain that they were not first timers. In fact, they had met at least a dozen couples, but never met anyone twice. It wasn't hard to figure out why. They were terrified of catching Aids, and would only do it with protection – no problem there – and preferred separate rooms – okay by us. So, after another half an hour of painful conversation and no sign of the offer of a drink, Marie finally dispensed with the niceties.

"Ok," she announced, "who's for the bedroom and who's for the settee?" They had already told us that their spare room was full of junk, so as usual I had to make do on the settee with the lady of the house.

The mind numbing conversation of the last one and a half hours had snapped Marie's patience, which is paper thin at the best of times, and she had gone into Dom mode.

"Right Tom," she said, "time to show me your etchings."

"Etchings?" said Tom looking bemused. Marie walked up to him, grabbed his crotch and led him out of the room.

"Fuck it," she said, "I'll show you mine instead."

Tom shuffled out of the lounge and up the stairs, Marie's grip tightening all the time. He turned just once as they left the room, the look on his face a mixture of pain and fear. I had to stifle a smile. Tom was going to learn a bitter lesson tonight. Don't make Marie angry – he wouldn't like her when she's angry.

I turned to Lyn. She was still sitting in the arm chair by the window. She was a reasonably attractive woman around the forty mark, but her old fashioned hair style and outdated clothes let her down, and being married to a deadbeat like Tom would hardly be invigorating. I decided to lay some of my devastating charm on her. I walked over, bent down and kissed her full on the lips whilst cupping her head in my hands, I felt her shiver and she gave a small gasp, I then knelt down in front of her and gently undid her cardigan – yes, you heard me, a cardigan, with little pink flowers and buttoned to the neck.

As I slowly undid every button Lyn began to breath in short sharp open mouthed bursts always a sure sign that a woman is getting turned on, when I had finished the cardigan I started on her blouse, which was also buttoned up to her neck. Another seventeen buttons later I was finally down to her bra, I couldn't be bothered fumbling around the back for the bra catch so I pulled the bra up over her boobs, as they were released Lyn gave a gasp and launched herself at me knocking me over backwards onto the living room floor. She was like a woman possessed as she threw herself on top of me pushing her boobs into my face and furiously rubbing my crotch. I hadn't expected this; she had gone from cold fish to hot potato in a matter of seconds. She now had one of her nipples stuffed into my mouth and was shouting,

"Bite it, bite it!" at the top of her voice. I duly obliged and she screamed in pleasure. This was great, all the waiting and naff conversation had been worthwhile, she had thrust her hand down the front of my trousers by this time and was trying to drag my dick out without undoing my trousers or unzipping the front. I don't think she understood that my wedding tackle was actually connected to the lower part of my body and the only way they were coming out from the top of my trousers was if she ripped them off, and if I didn't do something quickly, that is exactly what would happen. I swiftly unbuckled my belt, unzipped and laid open the flaps of my fly. Lynn could now stop tugging and do the job properly. Now every guy out there will know what I mean when I say some women know how to wank a bloke, and some women don't. Lyn definitely belonged to the latter. As soon as she had my dick upright she proceeded with a death like grip to drag my foreskin down so hard it nearly tore before coming up over the head and almost off the top of the helmet, and then dragging the whole lot down again slamming the base of her fist into my balls. This she did a dozen times before I could take no more. With all my strength I managed to roll her over and pin her arms to the floor. Lyn obviously loved sex but had never learned the art of sex, so my plan now was to dispense with the foreplay, or at least her version of it, and get down to some serious shagging, hopefully with me in control. With her arms still being held down I lowered my head next to her ear.

"Are you ready for some cock?" I whispered.

"Yes, yes!" she gasped, "But we need to use some protection."

"Don't worry," I said, "I have some condoms with me."

"No it's ok," said Lyn, "I have my own protection I always use."

"Ok," I said, "no problem."

Lyn slowly rolled over and, reaching under an arm chair, pulled out a flat, square box.

My God, I thought, it's a pizza. She wants to eat pizza in the middle of a sex session! She slowly opened the lid and lifted out a round dinner plate sized object, pale brown in colour.

No, it's not a pizza after all. It's a frisbee. Now she wants to start playing with a Frisbee.

"It's a femidom," said Lynn. "A female contraceptive. Its only been out about a year. I never use anything else. It gives total protection."

From what? A nuclear attack? She held it up for my inspection. It was about 9 inches across and made from thick, brown rubber with a sort of saggy bit in the middle. All it needed was a stick, and it could have been one of those giant novelty lollypops you get at the seaside. As I stood there looking at this Frisbee-sized slab of brown rubber, I was totally dumbfounded. In fact I didn't know whether to suck it, fuck it or throw it.

Now femidoms today are delicate gossamer thin things designed to give maximum sensitivity to both the man and woman, but this was the early nineties and this was the mark one version, the prototype where finesse and sensitivity had not been a design requirement in its manufacture. No, it was built to be functional and that's exactly what it turned out to be, clearly the man who had designed it had never had a shag, at least not with a woman, he may have had the odd fling with an Alaskan moose, or once been engaged to a grizzly bear, how else could you explain how someone could manufacture a sexual implement which had all the sensitivity of a snow plough.

Lyn lay down and spread the femidom on her pubic area, it covered all her lower belly and most of her inner thighs, she then pushed the saggy bit inside her.

"And it's washable!" she beamed, as though that would be a plus point with me.

"Oh good!" I replied, as I imagined it being hung over the washing line in the back yard and hosed down ready for the next guy, an image not conducive with my continued hard on. Earlier in the evening Lyn had said they had already met a dozen couples, that meant I would be the thirteenth guy to stick his dick into this abomination, another mental image guaranteed to kill the moment. Never the less, I manfully inched forward, cock in hand, determined not to be beaten by a round slab of rubber. As I neared this black hole and peered into the abyss I had only one thought on my mind, and that was to do the dastardly deed and get out quick.

"Lubrication," I said, "that's what we need, lubrication." Lyn reached across and passed me a huge tub of KY-jelly.

"This is ok," she said. "The manufacturers say not to use baby oil, as it will rot the rubber." Not a chance, I thought. That thing could hold sulphuric acid.

"Really?" I said. "Just goes to show!" I took a huge dollop of KY and pushed it into the inner recess of the femidom, it disappeared without a trace, another dollop went the same way, and another. I had all but emptied the tub when Lyn whispered,

"Now! I want it, now!"

"Then you shall have it now," I answered, as I shut my eyes and thought of England. I didn't need to fit it in I just thrust forward and my dick hit rubber and was funnelled to the centre and down into the fathomless depths. As my cock went in, a huge surge of KY-jelly came out accompanied by a loud squelching sound. KY had shot up onto my chest and arms and onto Lyn's boobs. I tried to wipe it off with my hands but only succeeded in spreading it over most of our bodies. We began to slide off each other and to add to our woes, every time I thrust into her, there was a terrible farting noise. As the air was expelled, it sounded like a whoopee cushion on the end of a pair of bellows. Remnants of the KY were still being splattered around and, all in all, the whole thing had turned into a disaster.

After one last, farty thrust I could carry on no longer. I slid off Lynn and lay on my back on the floor. Lyn lay there seemingly traumatised by it all. I heard a sort of slurping noise and turned just in time to see the glistening femidom slide out of Lyn and drop onto the floor between her legs, she didn't move; just gave a little high pitched squeak as it plopped out, and carried on staring at the ceiling. After what seemed like an eternity, Lyn sat up and looked at the femidom lying between her legs.

"Too much KY-jelly," she said.

"Too much rubber" I replied.

It took us about half an hour to clean up, by which time Marie and Tom had re-appeared. As we drove back home over the high moorland I recounted my first experience with a female contraceptive to Marie. Tears of laughter were still streaming down her face as we descended into the outskirts of Sheffield.

By a strange irony, the headlines of the local paper that night read *"Unidentified flying disc seen over Pennines."*

"I knew it!" I said, "it was a Frisbee after all."

"No," laughed Marie, "it's the mysterious case of the flying femidom." I had to chuckle to myself.

"I wonder if it left a trail of KY-jelly" I said.

No one ever found out what flew over the hills that night … but I have my suspicions.

CHAPTER 13

The Year of Hell

I am not, by nature, a pessimist, but if I have learned anything over the years its that life never runs smooth for long, and usually the time to worry is when things seem to be going great. That's when you are at your most vulnerable. That's when life can knock you for six, and that is how it was for Marie and me in 1993.

We were rolling along quite happily, the kids were all but grown up with the turbulent early teenage years behind them they both had decent, steady boyfriends. Vicky, the eldest, was carving out a career in childcare – a job she loved – and the youngest, Mandy, was teaching youngsters to ride at a horse riding school. We had bought her a pony a few years earlier and it had become her passion, so much so that the local riding stables had given her a job training the newcomers.

Our shoe business gave us a good living after many years of hard work and we had settled back into the lifestyle after our break and were meeting new friends as well as enjoying time with our old ones. So all in all, things were looking good.

It began to go seriously wrong in February. A phone

call in the early hours of the morning woke us abruptly from our sleep, and when the phone rings at that time of the morning it can only be bad news. A cold hand gripped my heart as I listened to Marie on the phone.

"We'll come now" she said. "Yes, we'll be there as quickly as possible." She had turned deathly white. "It's my mum. They've rushed her into hospital. That was the ward sister. She said to get there as soon as we can."

Five minutes later, we were in the car heading for the hospital. Marie's mum had been suffering from stomach problems recently, but she had been for numerous scans and x-rays and had been told there was nothing to worry about. They said it was probably a minor infection that would settle down eventually. Now, as we sped through the deserted early morning streets, neither of us could figure out what was happening. At the hospital, Marie's dad met us at the side ward door.

"Thank God you're here!" he said. "She took bad at home earlier and got steadily worse as the night wore on." He stopped for a minute to regain his composure. "I called the doctor and he sent her straight in. They've done lots of tests, but I can't find out anything."

"Dad, don't worry. We'll sort it" said Marie, trying to sound calm.

Marie's mum was lying in the bed, with tubes and drips all over her. She was barely conscious and seemed to be delirious. She was normally a lively, bubbly, outgoing woman, the life and soul of any family gathering, so to see her like this was a shock. Marie ran to her side, while I went to find some answers. In the corridor outside I ran into the staff nurse and a white coated doctor hurrying towards me. After confirming I was a member of the family the staff nurse told me the tests they had taken confirmed their suspicions. Marie's mum had full-blown septicaemia.

"What can you do?" I asked.

"If only we had got to her earlier..." said the doctor.

"You mean..."

"Yes," he answered, "I'm so sorry."

Marie's mum died in her arms an hour later, Marie whispering in her ear, "I love you mum" over and over as she passed away. I stood by her side feeling helpless. A lovely woman had just died and the injustice of it almost crushed me. It was all too sudden, too horrible to take in, like a terrible nightmare that you think you will wake from any minute.

Marie's family were devastated. Marie walked around in a daze for the next few days seemingly unable to accept what had happened, but slowly the realisation of her mother's death kicked in and the outpouring of grief almost overwhelmed her. Somehow we carried on, like zombies, just going through the motions, one day at a time, trying to come to terms with what had happened. Like a boxer who had just received a knock down punch, we fought to keep our senses, to maintain some kind of cohesion in our lives, but just as we were pulling ourselves groggily to our feet, fate bludgeoned us with another monstrous blow.

Three weeks after Marie's mum's death, my own mother was diagnosed with breast cancer. It was another horrendous shock. I immediately made an appointment to see the specialist. In his office he produced a chart with the outline of a woman and proceeded in a very clinical way to point out where the cancer was and where it had spread. It was all very matter of fact to him, he had done this a hundred times before. He droned on about lymph nodes and thyroid glands. I was listening but not taking it in. Was he telling me my mother was going to die?

"What's the prognosis?" I asked.

"She has one year, maybe less" he said glibly, then, almost as an afterthought, added, "It's very sad."

Sad? I thought, fucking sad? I wanted to stand up and scream at him.

"This is my mother you're talking about. This is the woman who gave me life, who kissed me better when I hurt my knee, who nursed me through whooping cough and mumps. This is the woman who gave me the last shillings out of her purse when I was desperate to go on a school trip, who told me bed time stories and taught me the words to *Run Rabbit Run*. This is the woman who got me my first bike and cried when I fell off and hurt my arm, the woman who never let me down, was always there even when I messed up, who's smile could make everything better and who loved me unconditionally. This woman whose gentle nature could sooth any angry moments, whose sacrifice to her family was beyond anything we could ever repay, whose love for us was total and without end. This is my mother, and you say it's sad, I'll give you fucking sad you bastard."

This is what I wanted to say, but instead I shook his hand, thanked him for his time and left his office.

My mother died in July, five months after Marie's mum. A gentle soul, who had never done anyone any harm had been taken. Now it was my family's turn to be devastated. I remember a feeling of rage sweeping over me. I wanted to lash out at a world that lets the passing of decent people go unnoticed while giving the dregs of society the care and nourishment they do not deserve, I wanted to rage against the hypocrisy of religious leaders, all the religions who preach frugality and obedience while they become rich on the backs of others. I wanted to rage against a political system that lets a woman struggle all her life to bring up a family with little or no help from the state, but sends criminals on holiday to rehabilitate them. I was angry for a long time after my mother died. I was forty three years old but felt like a child again. I had lost my mum and nothing could bring her back. My mother had been sixty-seven when she passed away, Marie's mum only sixty four. Both were taken well before their time, and both left a huge hole in our lives, that can never be filled.

We ground out the next few months, staggering from one task to the next, not thinking too much. Thinking brings pain and sometimes the pain is too much to bear.

We met Danny and Sue a few weeks after my mum's funeral, not for sex – that was unthinkable – but just to talk. Danny had lost his dad in Ireland a few years earlier and knew what we were going through. It helped me enormously to open up to him and Marie had a literal shoulder to cry on in Sue. Dave and Rachel were equally supportive, Dave had lost both his parents in the space of six months in the mid-eighties.

"It almost finished me, Baz," he said, "I was forty years old and I felt like an orphan. Like I was a little kid who had been abandoned." Marie and I both nodded in agreement. "But what helped me through was knowing what they would have wanted, and that is for us to live life to the full, make every day count and enjoy life. Isn't that what every parent wants for their child?" He was right, of course. Both our mums would have wanted us to carry on, and do the best for ourselves and our kids, so that is what we did our best to do.

By November of 1993 we could not wait for the year to end. The tragedies that had cursed us in that year had all but destroyed us, but life goes on and we saw the end of the year as a kind of end to the misery and a chance to start again. Little did we know that, in another part of the world, events were already transpiring to deal us another sickening blow. The year of hell had not finished with us yet.

Since the fall of the Berlin Wall there had been a huge mind shift in the Eastern European bloc. New ideas and new ways of dealing with the West had brought a kind of prosperity to the Eastern European nations. They were now consumers, just like the rest of us, and eager for things like clothes, cars, food... and shoes.

In November, we were told by the British Shoe Corporation in Leicester that the consignment of shoes we were due to pick up had, in fact, been shipped to East Germany. It was the beginning of the end; slowly, over time, all the contracts we had built up with British Shoe were taken over by Eastern European companies. It wasn't sudden, and we still kept other contracts we had with smaller shoe manufacturers, but the writing was on the wall, and the November knock back from British Shoe was the forerunner to the eventual downfall of our business – a business we had worked for the last thirteen years to build.

We had precious little to celebrate that Christmas, but we went through the motions anyway. Both our mums would have wanted it that way, but as I lay in bed on Christmas night my mind turned the last twelve months over and over in my head. The more I thought about it, the more depressed I became. What would become of us? I felt too old to start a new business. The last year had knocked the stuffing out of us.

We had no fight left.

Then a strange thing happened. As I lay there wrapped in my cocoon of misery I heard my mother's voice. It was unmistakably that soft, gentle voice I knew so well.

"Don't worry, Son. All things come to pass. Something will turn up, you'll see."

From me being a small child to an adult, she had said these words to me whenever I had a problem. I turned to Marie, feeling sure that she must have heard it, but she was fast asleep. Was it my imagination? I don't know, but one thing I do know is that mum was right. All things do come to pass, and something did turn up.

CHAPTER 14

La Chambre is Born

Marie and I gazed up at the rundown old building, the windows were shuttered up and the double fronted doors bolted and chained. It had once been a thriving pub in the east end of Sheffield, a welcoming watering hole for the thousands of thirsty steelworkers who lived and worked in the area. It was known as the Robin Hood and stood on the busy Attercliffe Road, a main arterial route in and out of the East End. Built in 1903, it had seen two world wars and countless booms and recessions, it was once surrounded by huge factories and 24 hour steel mills that belched acrid smoke and grime into the air and lit the night sky orange and red when the vast furnaces tapped out. Its clientele were hard working, hard drinking foundry men, tough men who would fight with bare knuckles in the street over a spilt beer, but would share their last shilling with the family next door.

This was the backdrop to the Robin Hood pub in the twenties and thirties and pre war years. After the war it was boom time again and in the fifties and sixties the huge steelworks were all working to capacity, employment was high and the Robin Hood, like many pubs in the area, was packed day and night by the shift workers, but by the late seventies and early eighties recession was biting again and this time the old pub would not survive, and by 1987, it closed its doors as a pub for the last time. It was now 1997; the old building had lain boarded up and derelict for ten years. As Marie and I looked at its blackened walls, its leaking roof and general state of disrepair, we began to have our doubts, could this really be our next business venture, could we take this old worn out building and drag it screaming and kicking into the new millennium, it was like a dinosaur stuck in a by-gone age, all the old steelworks had gone, torn down to make room for a new shopping centre and retail parks with their MacDonalds and Pizza Huts, monuments to a new age. The Robin Hood stood amongst this new growth like a memorial to a forgotten time, a simpler time, it did not seem possible that we could use this old decrepit building steeped so much in the past to function for such a radical new idea. What we had planned would not only bring the place into modern day, but some would say our plans were even futuristic. But we are jumping ahead here; to make sense of it we have to go back four years.

We had just been through the year of hell, when both our dear mothers had passed and our shoe retail business had begun to crumble, try as we might we could not save it. Most of the shoes we bought were end of lines, over makes or seconds, but now these were being snapped up by the Eastern Europeans and even some African nations. I remember travelling down to Shorditch High Street in London to look at a consignment of mixed footwear at a knock down price.

When we got there the owner of the factory took us to an old warehouse across the street which was filled with second hand shoes (known as worn returns), there must have been ten thousand pairs, the vast majority of them beyond repair and only fit for the bin, when we told the owner we would have to pick out the best pairs he shrugged his shoulders and said he could shift the whole lot to the Nigerian government for £1.00 per pair. When we pointed out that they were mostly garbage he told us he knew that, but they would buy them strip them all down to the base components and make a third of them into wearable shoes for the Nigerian public, it seems they did not mind wearing a pair of shoes consisting of a sole from a Doc Martin, uppers from a pair of ladies sandals and laces from old trainers. They had cheap manpower to convert them, and best of all the public who bought them weren't fashion conscious.

"Sounds like the perfect combination to me" said the factory owner.

It became increasingly difficult to buy decent stock at the right price, instead of one trip we were making dozens of smaller trips to maintain supplies, running costs quadrupled and profits nose-dived, and by the summer of 1996 we knew our best efforts could not sustain us and our business was doomed. We closed down the wholesale warehouse (how could we supply others when we could hardly supply ourselves?) and sold off two of the vans. We had to lay off Marie's brother who had worked for us for over five years, and now we just had our solitary shoe shop. I suppose, luckily for us, both our daughters had left home. Vicky was married to Craig, who was to become an integral part of our club in later years. And

Mandy later married Jonathan who, as I write, is our car park supervisor, so we only had to maintain the two of us. But it was not easy-going without the luxuries we had become accustomed to over the last few years. Financially we were back where we began when the kids were small and I had left my job in the steelworks to start my own business, but I wasn't thirty any more, I was forty six and, at this point in my life, I had neither the energy nor the enthusiasm to start over.

Our salvation, although we did not know it at the time, lay close at hand. In all the books I have ever read and all the television programs I have ever seen the same message has always come through. When starting a business from scratch, stick to what you know. It may seem obvious enough now, but ten years ago the idea of opening a swingers' club was tantamount to opening a drinking club in Chicago in the prohibition era. So we ploughed on, ignoring the obvious. The shoe shop paid the bills, but only just, and it did not warrant two of us working there. So leaving Marie in the shop I took to driving around looking for places where we could set up another business. I came across the Robin Hood pub, but discounted it as being too big for our needs, I was still stuck in retailing mode. This went on for two or three months. We were getting nowhere fast.

Then one day, we found ourselves in Blackpool. We had gone to meet a couple called Mike and Babs, who we had met once before at a house party. They had invited us over for the weekend, and suggested we go to a local pub which held swingers' events in the room upstairs. We had been to places like this before. It was usually a large function room with a makeshift disco at one end. There would be tables and chairs spread around and a small clearing for anyone who wanted a dance. If you were really lucky there would be a toilet upstairs, but most of the time you had to go downstairs to use the loo and, of course, buy your drinks, which always brought stares and cat calls from the regulars in the bar. This place was no different, except someone had laid on a buffet and put a small television with a video recorder in the corner showing blue films.

"They must have smuggled that in past the landlord," joked Mike. "Why can't people watch what they want to watch?" he continued.

"Don't get me started." I said. "It's riled me for years how some do-gooder, sat in their ivory tower, can tell you and me what we can and can't watch on telly, or even do in places like this." I looked around. A few women were dancing topless, but that was it, there were no facilities for them to take things further, there were no cloakrooms, no bar, not even their own toilet – just a bare room where they had to hide the telly with the blue film. They were treated like second-class citizens.

"What if someone were to open a proper club with proper facilities?" I said to Mike.

"They'd be arrested." he replied. "No authority in the land would stand for it. They would be shut down quicker than you can say 'Get your tits out!'" he laughed. Mike was right, the few gatherings like this that got too high profile were quickly closed down by the police. But the more I thought about it the more I became convinced it was the way forward.

I could feel the old enthusiasm flooding back, as we drove home over the Pennines the following day. I had told Marie of my plan as we left Blackpool and we were still discussing it as we descended on the Yorkshire side of the M62.

"It can't work," she protested. "No one has managed to open one of these clubs without being raided and closed down."

"That's because they're not doing it right." I said. "They're trying to duck and dive. We'll do it by the book, everything above board."

"Do you really think it will be that easy?" she said.

"Of course not, but we'll take it one step at a time, tackle each hurdle as it comes. What have we got to lose?" Marie cupped her chin in her hand.

"Err, let me think. How about our money, what little we have? Our reputation, when it hits the papers? To say nothing of our freedom, when we get locked up!"

She had a point. If the powers that be wanted to make an example of us there were a whole range of charges that could be levied, many of them carrying mandatory prison sentences. It had happened to others who had tried for much less grander plans than ours. I tried to lighten the mood.

"Well, look at it this way – if we go down, you'd at least end up in a women's prison, so you can still have your fun, whereas I will probably end up as somebody's bitch," Marie laughed.

"Now that could be worth it – you getting what you've been giving out all these years!"

"I don't think being rear-ended by some big hairy con is comparable to the pleasure I have dispensed to the women of this fine country for the last few years thank you!"

For now the discussion had ended on a light note, but it would continue over the next few days, until an agreement was reached between us to at least view the Robin Hood and see if it was a viable location, which brings us back to where we came in at the beginning of this chapter.

We unlocked the old rusty padlock to the front door and stepped inside, peering through the gloom, we could make out a bar, tables and chairs strewn around and a pool table that had obviously seen better days. Dust and decay were everywhere and the vandals had done their work.

"This will take thousands," said Marie.

"I reckon twenty-five should do it," I said. "Thirty, tops." I was being deliberately under-budget. In reality, it would probably take fifty-thousand pounds to convert this place into the kind of club we wanted, and remember this was 1997 prices.

That night at home we weighed up our options. They were limited, to say the least. I could go back to the steelworks, but there were precious few left and it was mostly high-tech specialised stuff. It had been sixteen years since I worked in them, now they would be an alien environment. I would have to start at the bottom again on a minimum wage and, apart from that, I was used to being the boss now. I didn't know if I could start taking orders again at my age.

Marie had done a course in touch-typing when she was younger, but the money that paid would not keep petrol in the car, let alone pay the bills.

Of course, we knew about shoes, we knew about the latest trends and next season's colours. Even today, I can look at a woman's feet and tell her her shoe size – I'm seldom wrong. I can do it with men too, but it's not as much fun. But, for all our knowledge on the subject, this was the time of the big cut-price shoe chains, the huge discount warehouses and the eastern block nations clambering for anything they could lay their hands on. Small independent traders such as ourselves were going out of business at a phenomenal rate.

No, it always came back to the same thing. The only other thing we knew was swinging. We had been doing it for seventeen years. We knew the scene inside and out – not only knew it, but had done it, lived it, well and truly bought the t-shirt.

So the die was cast and I opened a bottle of cheap wine to celebrate. Looking back, if we had known the trials and hardships, to say nothing of the sleepless nights and stomach churning anxiety that awaited us, I doubt we would have even attempted it. But in our blissful naivety, we walked into the minefield by opening a high profile swingers' club in 1997.

We had so many things to do. Arrange finance, organise builders, draw up plans, run adverts, contact authorities, etc. etc., the list seemed endless.

"There's one thing we haven't done," I said.

"What?" asked Marie

"Find a name for the club." I answered. "What about *Sex R Us*?"

"Mm, I don't think so," said Marie. "French is a sexy language... what about *Le Parisian*?" she added.

"What about the *Oh La La Club*?" I laughed.

"I've got it!" she said. "*La Chambre*!"

"What's that mean?" I asked.

"If I remember my French from school, it means the bedroom."

"I still think *Sex R Us* is better," I said.

"*La Chambre* it is then!" announced Marie.

It was, and has been ever since, but this is not the end of the story. There is one more book in this trilogy – about the club and, more importantly, the people in it.

We thought we had seen it all, but running a swingers' club for the last ten years has opened even our eyes. It taught us you never stop learning and, if you think you're shock proof, think again.

There were the national newspaper exposés, the television programmes, the gangs at the door, the police, the council, the incredible sex lives of some of the people we have met, the...

But hold on, I'm getting ahead of myself. I have to put it all in some sort of order, so if you will excuse me, I have to go and open the club with Marie, and if it's not too wild tonight, and if I'm not too tired tomorrow, I will begin writing *Swingers 3*.